Once Upon the Rhine

Cody the Cockatrice Series

Book One

RA ANDERSON

ra-anderson.com
myfavoritebookspublishingco@gmail.com
My Favorite Books Publishing Company, LLC.
Kingston, Georgia USA

Ordering Information:

Quantity sales. Special discounts are available on quantity purchases by corporations, associations, and others. Orders by U.S. trade bookstores and wholesalers. For details, contact the publisher at the address above.

Painting by Lindsey Wilson
Cody the Cockatrice Sketches by Hannah Jones
Other Sketches and Photography by RA Anderson
Hypertrophic Cardiomyopathy information curtesy of www.4HCM.org
Editing by The Pro Book Editor
Interior and Cover Design by IAPS.rocks

ISBN: 978-1-950590-19-3

1. Main category—JUVENILE FICTION/Animals/Dragons, Unicorns & Mythical
2. Second category—JUVENILE FICTION/Readers/Chapter Books
3. Third Category—JUVENILE FICTION/Fantasy & Magic

First Edition

Books by RA Anderson

Once Upon the Rhine
(Cody The Cockatrice Series Book One)

The Last Crabtree Girl

Girl Sailing Aboard the Western Star

Puffins Take Flight
(Iceland: The Puffin Explorers Book 1)

Puffins Off the Beaten Path
(Iceland: The Puffin Explorers Book 2)

Puffins Encounter Fire and Ice
(Iceland: The Puffin Explorers Series Book 3)

Iceland: The Puffin Explorers Book of Fun Facts

If Pets Could Talk: A Service Dog

If Pets Could Talk: Dogs

If Pets Could Talk: Cats

If Pets Could Talk: Farm Animals

For Cody, Cassaundra, Brody & Zane

CHAPTER ONE

Meet Cody

"One, two, three,

gray, cracked cobblestones pass
beneath these little rooster feet;

Four, five, six,

my dragon wings and tail casting
shadows on the bricks;

Seven, eight, nine,

with each small stride I'm counting
the steps along the Rhine;

Ten, eleven, twelve,

Cody the Cockatrice is alive and well!"

I WAS WANDERING AROUND THE STREETS of Basel, Switzerland, as I had for the past thousand years or so, but that day was not like any other day. It was my invisible birthday. Yep, exactly fifty years of being invisible to humans. My so-called invisible birthday began on the very day that all humans stopped believing in my magical powers, leaving me *invisible*.

The huge lump in my throat was nothing. I'm a mean, lean, child-protecting cockatrice-godparent. My eyes had dust in them, that's all. My hands quivered, and I shook, but not from heartache or even being lonely. I am stronger than that!

Heat rose from my rooster toes to the very top feather on my head, and my brawny chest expanded with a huff and a puff. When I'm upset, I count...

"Thirteen, fourteen, fifteen...

"I will count louder! That should help! I can scream if I want because no human can hear nor see me."

So maybe I was a little upset about being invisible. As my rage grew, my small featherless wings fluttered enough to lift me off my feet from time to time. Then I stomped so hard my feet pulsed with pain. Anger bubbled inside me like molten lava in an active volcano, and my orange feathers flared a brilliant red. I couldn't hold it in any longer. The top of my head split, and my blue eyes reddened and turned to black holes swallowed by darkness.

My dragon wings expanded and fell flat and ruffled about out of control as I counted every stone in town, trying to calm myself.

Instead of unleashing my rage, I'd decided to count and walk it off. It was the smart thing to do!

"Sixteen, seventeen, eighteen…"

I stomped up and down the narrow cobble-stoned streets of Basel, trying to remember why I'd chosen this town from the thousands of places I could have gone—Rome, Paris, London…any-where in Europe. As if I had no control over my feathers at this point of madness, they ruffled and my throat grumbled as I spat out these words: "Boring is what boring does," my mother used to say. But no one had been able to see me in more than fifty years, and I was bored out of my mind, I tell you!

I thought only a few of us cockatrice-godparents still existed after the invention of games with mythological beasts. We cockatrice-godparents (CGP) had run out of believers. Without our guardian children, our kind simply shrank. I was fearful that my days were numbered before I too would go with the other cockatrice into the great unknown. Seriously, I didn't know what had happened to them. It was like they'd vanished.

"Oh, my! Are we going extinct?" I'd said aloud, stopping suddenly. "I am a cockatrice! An extraordinary hybrid cockerel-dragon, protector of guardian children. A cockatrice is fathered by a rooster, mothered by a lizard, and hatched by a toad. We are the true little blood cousins of dragons. We inherited their wings and tails, you know!

"One hundred three, one hundred four, one hundred five... Wait, I lost track again. One, two, three... We are strong and brave! Don't let this eight-inch body fool you. An ant can lift 5,000 times his weight, but a cockatrice is 5,000 times stronger than a human!" I resumed walking along the river. "Four, five, six..."

With an effortless three-foot vertical hop—BAM!—I landed on the ledge of a little pool of water with a statue in the middle. If you can believe it, humans made statues of us and placed them all over their city. Yes, statues. Cockatrices in fierce warrior poses looked over humans' valuable water fountains on nearly every Basel city block. A steady stream of water showered downward from a small pipe placed in the mouth of a bronzed cockatrice, and they called it a water fountain.

I shook the water off my feathers and stepped away to avoid the water spilling from the mouth of the evil-looking cockatrice. It's been a long fifty years, and sometimes I found myself speaking to the cockatrice statues.

"Wait, they think we are mythological beasts. How stupid! This is clearly why children don't believe in us anymore! Why am I talking to a bronzed cockatrice statue?"

As I'd watched this little town grow, the past fifty years had crept...and I mean time was really slow. It was worse than watching glue dry, far worse than watching paint dry or waiting for water to boil. It was worse than waiting for a school day to end. That's how slow time was passing. Where are all the cockatrices going? Maybe I didn't want to know. Lately, I had not searched for my brothers and sisters, not wanting to miss my opportunity to find a guardian child.

Bam! I was back down to the cobblestone. I loved doing that! I couldn't control it! My feathers raged red again. It was getting harder to control my temper—my frenzy. Most of all, this counting kept my eyes from dripping warm liquid down my cheeks. Humans called it crying, but I was not a crybaby! I wanted to walk and count and follow this road to nowhere.

"...one-hundred-three, one-hundred-four, one-hundred-five..."

Looking up, I noticed a family waiting for a bus. A teenager looked down at his phone, not paying attention to anything else. Another child had her nose stuck between two pages of a book. More books had been written, and we—the cockatrice—were again portrayed as evil characters. Even the most popular children's book in the world had us portrayed as crazy beasts.

I'd watched children with their noses pressed into those Harry Potter books. I found out that in some 1792 Triwizard Tournament, one of the tasks was to capture a cockatrice. Most humans had blurred the facts between the mythological creature and the real cockatrice. That's what I thought. I don't know if my sisters or brothers had found children who believed, but I wondered where they'd gone. Where was everyone? I wandered the streets of Basel bored out of my mind, without a guardian child to protect.

The last time I'd visited my brother Daniel in Köln had been more than twenty-five years before, and my brother Sem in Heidelberg, Germany, had been about ten years before. My sister Pia lived near the Strasbourg Cathedral de Notre Dame. It had only been forty-five-ish years since I had visited with her. It had been maybe five or six years since I had spoken with my brother Finn, who lived in Holland—oh, that's right. It was renamed the Netherlands. The last time I had seen my sister Clara in Germany—in the Black Forest—was maybe, uh… Oh, my. Well, forty or so years before. What if they had vanished like the rest of the cockatrice? What would I do? I knew I needed to find a guardian child before I disappeared!

I didn't think there was one child who believed. If children didn't believe, a cockatrice couldn't be seen.

"Why can't any child see me? Why am I *invisible!*"

My feathers then turned fiery red, and smoke

rose to follow me. A lump formed in my throat, but the only thing I could do was shake it off!

My top speed was about 100 miles per hour.

"That's it! I will fly this madness off! I will count rooftops! One, two, three..."

CHAPTER TWO

Meet Brody

L IFTING MY BACKPACK INTO MOM'S van was more than a challenge. It was like lifting a ton of bricks. Mom grabbed it from me because she didn't like my lifting anything too heavy because of my heart condition. She thinks she's helping me but it's the most upsetting thing anyone could do to me in public. The only thing I can do is let go, so I did. I walked away but when I did this, my face felt flushed, and I could feel my heart beat in my chest. Then not knowing if it's my heart issue or being upset, it is such a fine line, the only thing I can do is go bury my head in a book and escape this life. So, that's what I did.

I was loaded down with artwork, papers, unused school supplies, and my most prized possessions, the whole Harry Potter series, and those weigh a lot. Well, another school year was over, and I couldn't wait to be a fourth grader. My classroom next school year would be closer to the library, and we would share the big playground with the fifth graders. Hopefully, we wouldn't play at the same time as the older kids because my brother Bowen would be in the fifth-grade class.

Ever since I was diagnosed with hypertrophic cardiomyopathy, HCM for short, it has limited me from team sports. I had to leave behind my soccer team. I can participate in PE as long as it's not a timed mile run or a competitive soccer or basketball game. It's not that I'm not capable. It's because of my heart thing. Basically, my heart is abnormally thick with no apparent cause, and athletics can cause the heart to thicken suddenly, causing it not to work like it should. I will have HCM my whole life. Some people are born with it, some people have it and are eighty years old. It's not like it's keeping me from life, only from being a professional soccer player, and that wasn't my dream anyway. I would like to be a computer software developer or maybe an engineer.

I didn't mind not being able to play team sports. Much. But it's why I dove into piano lessons more, plus I now play golf with my dad and have more time to ride horses with my mom.

Well, maybe it would be cool to have Bowen around the playground so the other kids would understand. Bowen was the sports jock in the family. The best day for him was a full day on the playground or at PE, but the best day of my third grade was the day I spent practically all day in the library. It was the first day I discovered the Harry Potter books.

After I read the first few chapters or so, I had

begun to get really hungry. As I walked around the small library, I noticed my class was gone. I looked out the window toward the sound coming from outside. It was Bowen's class following the PE teacher to the gym. That was normally his last class of the day, but I thought perhaps they'd changed it that day.

I walked up to Mrs. Glass, the school's librarian, and asked how much longer until lunch. When she looked up, she had a puzzled expression on her face, then she took me to the front office because I had missed lunch. She ended up driving me to get Chick-fil-A. Best school lunch ever!

After I ate lunch, the buses were headed home, and all the moms and dads who picked up were in line. It was the end of the school day, so I ended up not going to any of my classes. I had just read for most of the school day.

I'd always felt I had a knack of being undetectable and even stealth-like. It paid off being invisible that day! That by far was my best day in third grade!

Being the middle child was also much like being the invisible child. Bowen, my older brother, demanded all the attention. When he entered a room, it was like a bulldozer crashing into the walls. His voice was demanding, not obnoxious, but it was as though he bellowed out, "See me!" He was the same way on the soccer field, anywhere the coach put him. He was the star.

I'd heard kids on the opposing team say that hitting number twelve, Bowen, was like hitting a brick wall running at full speed. Bowen was always selected first on teams, and at the end of every school year, he was rewarded athletic recognition for top athletic ability.

Bryant, our baby brother, had this way of flashing his big blue eyes and giggling, which drew the attention of anyone and everyone around. Even though he had just finished kindergarten and wasn't a baby, he still had that cooing effect on every adult on the planet. He reminded me of a flower that naturally drew in all of Earth's bees.

I could walk into a room and exit, unheard and unseen. I didn't mind. This was the way it was and always had been. Mom used to say that I possessed the magical powers of a stealth-like being. If that was the case, I totally enjoyed the power of invisibility. When Mom parks the van in the garage, I will slip out and be in my room before Mom notices. Home sweet home.

***

I can officially call this day summer break! I had nowhere to rush off to and no brothers to dodge in the early morning rush. When I walked into the kitchen, Mom handed me some information about the Once Upon the Rhine cruise that our Fairy TripMother had sent us. Our Fairy Trip-Mother was really Mom's best friend. She had the best business ever, booking trips all over the world, mainly because she got to go check them out for herself all the time.

She'd booked us on this cruise after she cruised down the Seine River. We would be cruising on a ship that looked like a floating hotel on the Rhine River. It was convenient having the family computer in the kitchen, so I logged on and started researching the cities we would be visiting and located them on the map.

We lived in north Georgia, so we would leave from the Atlanta airport and arrive at our final destination in Basel, Switzerland, flying 4,641 miles. Basel is where Germany, France, and Switzerland meet. I once read that if you go out the wrong door at the airport you might end up in the wrong country.

The Rhine River, where we would take our cruise, ran up to the north on the map. It flowed down from the Swiss Alps and all the way to the North Sea. We would be floating with the river. It was the second longest river in Europe and important for the economy, exporting and importing products around the world, like Swiss chocolate and Swiss army knives. Along with the Swiss army knife, which happened to be invented in Switzerland, other inventions there included the potato peeler, Velcro (the original loop-and-hook fasteners), edible chocolate gold, and milk chocolate!

One particular famous person born in Basel

was Edwin Fischer, and there had been some or-
chestra performances where only the songs inter-
preted by Edwin Fischer were played. My piano
teacher once told me that Edwin Fischer was one
of the best interpreters of two of the most famous
piano players of all time: Mozart and Bach.

Mom was talking on the phone, and I overheard her telling someone that our journey would
start in Basel, Switzerland. Mom's statement
wasn't correct, but I didn't argue or worry about
it, because our journey started from home and
later would end at home. That's how I saw it! I
knew it would be a cool vacation, but I wished we
could teleport there.

As Mom hung up the phone, I slid away from
the computer, feeling the need to see why it was
so oddly quiet in the house. It was best to avoid
Mom on days like these. It was the safer way to
avoid chores.

I left my room and saw Mom hand Bowen a
packing list, asking him to go pack his suitcase.
She then walked into Bryant's room, grabbed a
suitcase, and started packing Bryant's clothes. At
my parents' bedroom door, I noticed Dad packing his bag, and he made it look easy. I always
thought he was so good at packing because he
traveled so much.

Before anyone noticed me, I snuck off to finish building our new Lego castle. "Hey, Bowen,"

I called out to my brother, "do you want to play a video game with me when you're done packing?"

Bowen nodded as he stuffed shirts and pants into his suitcase.

As I passed Mom and Dad's room, I overheard them talking to one another about how long the next day would be, which meant I was going to play while I could. It sure seemed like a lot of work to leave for a vacation.

Before the sun breached the horizon, noises traveled through the house, and suitcase wheels rolled across the maple wood floor. I was the first to grab the bathroom and wanted to be the first downstairs to eat breakfast. Mom was in the kitchen making breakfast for Bryant while tossing sandwiches and snacks into a reusable grocery sack. Dad exited with one bag before coming back to search for the next. Bowen was in his room slowly waking up, because no one liked to disturb him in the morning unless absolutely necessary.

My backpack, which was my one carry-on item, was ready, filled with as many books as I could find that I hadn't already read. I had also packed origami paper with a how-to book that I had received last Christmas. I added Lego guys in one of the front pockets and retrieved the Nintendo DS and Switch from charging. I stuffed the chargers to my electronics in the side pocket, then asked my dad for an American-to-European adapter.

Without an adapter, our American plugs would not fit or work with a European outlet. I knew Dad would have several since he traveled around the world for work. That was another thing I had learned reading our Once Upon the Rhine cruise trip itinerary, which contained a list of the places we were going and what we should pack.

Ready to go, I entered the kitchen and sat down to have breakfast as Dad walked in from loading our suitcases in the car. He asked Mom where my bag was, and I showed him my backpack. He shot a glance toward Mom. Her face flushed, and she hurried up the stairs. We could hear her walking above us, seemingly in a rush. As I finished eating, Mom appeared with my packed bag. I sometimes noticed Mom would forget to tell me to pack, but she seemed to do a lot of things for me, and sometimes I let her.

Bowen entered the room dressed, but his hair was flared up on one side resembling a pin wheel. He glared my way. That was the look he used to give right before I should have disappeared, so I did!

As my family scurried around the house readying to leave, I grabbed my backpack and got into the car. We had at least an hour-and-a-half drive to the airport, and I wanted to start reading. I hoped I would finish my book before we got to the airport so I wouldn't have to carry it around.

It was quiet in the car, and I wondered what was taking everyone so long to leave. The book was good, and it was nice to read before the car started moving and I had to listen to everyone talk.

Mom arrived with Bowen and Bryant, then rushed off to call for Dad. Apparently, they had been looking for me. The long ride to the airport was quieter than I expected.

Once we were settled on the plane, musical airplane seats were played throughout the flight to avoid conflict, fighting, and most of all, crying. Mom would sit between Bowen and me to play cards, then Dad would switch seats so we could watch a movie with him. During that time, Bryant and Mom played games and read a book together. Then we switched back so Mom and Dad could sit together.

The three of us watched several movies, like *Toy Story*, *Lion King*, *Frozen*, and *Abominable*. We wanted to watch *IT*, and we even begged Mom and Dad. Bowen and I claimed clowns were funny and we wouldn't be scared, but we didn't win. We ate our sandwiches that Mom had made—thank goodness, because airplane food was simply gross! We played video games, conquering several levels of *Donkey Kong* before moving on to a new game on the Switch.

Even though our eyes burned and our yawns were triggered by one another, we were not tired.

Mom had packed snacks, so we ate them. The intercom broke the silence, and the extremely loud captain's voice announced our arrival in Amsterdam. If we were tired, the blaring voice throughout the plane shook off our fatigue. But the glooming realization was that we had another flight after this one, and that made me feel almost grumpy and sick inside.

The customs line at the Amsterdam airport between flights didn't look long, but after an hour, we were only halfway through. The customs agent must have been taking extra time looking at everyone's passports. The thought of someone sneaking into the country illegally triggered an onset of tales and theories by my brothers and me, wondering why they would need to cross the border illegally. Our conspiracy stories were soon halted by both Mom and Dad.

The passports were stamped, and we made a mad dash to the next plane. The flight to Basel was entertaining, as Bowen and I watched the occasional head nods of Mom and Dad, but we soon found ourselves snoozing as we lay over one another like a pile of puppies.

The heavy bump of the airplane wheels hitting the runway jolted everyone awake. Dazed, we almost forgot where we were going. When the fog lifted from our minds and we heard an announcement made in German, we needed no translation. We knew we were close. Suddenly, we were wide awake and couldn't wait to explore Basel, Switzerland.

Exiting the plane was slow, as if we were moving through a dense haze, and it wasn't gone until we found the baggage claim. We followed the signs to Switzerland as we walked through the hallways of the airport with our suitcases in tow. Once outside, we found our airport transfer, which took us to our hotel. After we'd checked in and taken our luggage to the room, we headed out to explore. The street in front of the hotel was wide, providing lanes for cars and room for two trainlike tracks running down the center. Seconds after the green tram had vanished down the street, the wheels on the tracks screeched and air hissed when the double doors opened on a bright yellow tram. These trainlike public transport trams were painted and color-coded for people who traveled to different sections of the town, and numbers matched the area where each tram would stop. We boarded, found seats, and watched the old brick buildings slide past the windows as the tram started to move.

Day was night and night was day. We started to realize that we hadn't gone to bed for more than thirty-six hours, and another game of tag yawning began. My eyelids were heavy, but I didn't want to miss anything.

The tramway was the quickest way to get around town and a fast way to get familiar with the area and find some place to eat. My stomach grumbled more than once before the tram's sixth stop, so Mom and Dad decided we should get off at a stop near the Rhine River.

We proceeded to walk across the Mittlere Brücke, meaning "middle bridge," which was a regal old brick bridge probably built with royalty in mind. Flags from the bordering countries and Switzerland lined it, one on top of each pillar crossing the river. The Swiss flag reminded me of the red cross logo, but the flag is actually a white cross on a red square. I believe it is one of the two square flags in the world representing a country.

The bridge was only used by the tramway, bikes, or people on foot. A couple dozen people walked across. Some took pictures with the Swiss flag, and others floated underneath the bridge, down the Rhine River. A bell's occasional sharp ringing indicated that another tramway approached, and people leapt off the road and back onto the sidewalk.

We made our way back to a tramway car and rode it to the hotel. During the ride, my eyelids became heavier, my eyes stung when I opened them, and my head ached with pain.

We stopped and ate at a restaurant called the Union Diner, a strange name for a Swiss diner that sold hamburgers and french fries. It was really a great place to eat, and it made everyone happy.

I couldn't wait to continue exploring Basel tomorrow, but I couldn't wait to sleep even more.

CHAPTER THREE

Cody

I HAD HUGE DREAMS DURING MY years of training. I chose to live in Basel when others scoffed. It was no larger than ten square miles, so the other cities and towns dwarfed Basel in comparison, but there was something special about the town. I wanted to be a cockatrice-godparent (CGP) there. I felt how special this town was and how important it could be to the world.

I quickly flew up to the top of the Switzerland flagpole and perched in the middle of the Mittlere Brücke bridge to mess with some younger tourists trying to take a picture. Being bored, I sometimes did silly things. This particular bridge was built to sit in the town of Stein am Rhein. Fed by two lakes, along with the melting snow and ice from the top of the famous Swiss Alps, the Rhine River ran through—or passed by—several countries, including France, Germany, the Netherlands, and Switzerland.

I enjoyed watching the tourists. Sometimes when someone tried to take a picture with the Swiss flag, I made the flag flutter. This caused the flag to blur in their photograph. It made me laugh when they looked down and tried to figure it out, but that too got old. Another thing I liked to do was hang out on top of any of the dozens of water fountains with the bronzed cockatrice statues that were around town near the Rhine. I listened to the adults tell children about the mythological cockatrice, and I wondered why the adults had forgotten us and only referred to what they read.

Some of my former guardian children had grown up to be wonderful elder-humans. I could vividly remember Jacob Bernoulli, born in 1654; Johann Bernoulli, born in 1667; and Leonhard Euler, born in 1707, who were amazing mathematicians. Watching them was like seeing the inside of a calculator at work.

Arnold Böcklin, born in 1827, was a painter, sculptor, and a university teacher when he became a human-elder. As a little child, he was always making mud holes so he could create clay sculptures. He made the perfect sculpture of me once, and his mother stomped it back into the ground, saying his imagination was too big for his young self. My cousin was his mother's guardian. How could she have forgotten? I missed Johann, Jacob, little Leo, and Arnold. Those were the good old days.

I spent my days watching and waiting, perched up on the edge of a fountain and looking down into the water at my reflection, asking myself, "Why don't I have a guardian child? Why have all children chosen not to believe, when in fact so many need me?"

"Cody, the reason is…you are no longer liked or needed."

My heart skipped a beat. *Can I now hear my reflection talk?* I wondered.

A giggling howl let out behind me, and I reeled around to see who it was. My cousin, a dragon faerie named Freddy.

"It's not true, Freddy! I am liked. I was liked a lot!" I told him.

"Listen, Cody, you should probably find a new home. It's annoying having you mope around my town day after day for what…100 years now?" Freddy said.

"It's been fifty years by the way, not one hundred!" I corrected him.

"Oh, my bad!" Freddy said as he flew away as fast as he'd appeared.

"Maybe Freddy is right, maybe I should leave."

Daniella, my first faerie professor at the CGP academy, had told enchanting stories of this town, named Basilia back in the Roman times. After a while, the name had been mixed with Old French, English, and Icelandic, and it eventually became Basel. She spoke of a magical place where the Rhine River flowed all the way to the North Sea. Daniella had made this town sound magical. It was an amazing town until…the children stopped believing. Why?

"Oh, no, look at my feathers! They are turning red again. I am tired of counting, what else will help me forget?"

I was here when Basel was in the midst of bloody wars. I helped children survive battles, poverty, changes in leadership, and the deadly Great Plague. Oh, how I remembered that disease. I found myself staring at the bronzed statue again.

Hoping for an answer, I asked, "Were you here back in the mid-1300s, when the Black Plague was one of the most deadly and devastating pandemics in human history? Well, I was!"

The disease and all the deaths almost broke me. That was until I found how to keep the humans that carried the diseases away from one another to help prevent it from spreading further. All I had to do was keep them from breathing, sneezing, and coughing on one another. Some resisted. I don't know why. I couldn't help those.

I kept my guardian children separated, shielding them from germs and becoming a layer of personal protection by putting myself between the infected and my guardian child. I started to grab a cloth—any cloth—near us and cover myself, making it look like my guardian children had covered themselves. I taught other cockatrices to do the same, and after the parents realized those kids were not getting sick, the idea stuck. Some separated from one another, some that couldn't simply shielded themselves with layers of face protection.

After those life-changing events and after the infection was basically gone, several of my guardian children helped build Basel back from practically nothing. I can stand tall and proud thinking of those guardian children as elders, knowing what I helped them accomplish.

Suddenly it hit me! I knew what I needed to calm down—chocolate! Ya, it didn't have anything to do with anything I was talking about, but I remembered chocolate always made my children and me happy! I knew just where to go.

I flew above the cathedral and admired its beauty, deciding to sit there and wait. I loved that place. The tours always started there, or at least the important ones, like the cacao tours. Yes, chocolate tours. I'd made the cathedral my home after the children stopped believing. That was when I became invisible, jobless, and homeless.

Buildings in European countries were built to last hundreds and hundreds of years, perfect for a cockatrice since we lived for thousands of years. Most of the buildings had survived through battles, wars, and earthquakes, like this one—well, it had been fixed up a few times, but that gave it character!

This cathedral was built on the first settlement in Basel in the very place I lived, and they called it Cathedral Hill. I slept in the north tower the humans had named Georgsturm.

Because I was invisible, my home was anywhere I wanted it, but I liked the north tower for its view of the Rhine River. I would watch, hypnotized, as the river flowed north. Day and night, it was always peaceful and kept my mind from my unfortunate circumstances—you know, the invisible thing and not having anyone to look after.

In a matter of days, humans could take a bargelike ship from Basel to Amsterdam. Fresh water and traveling were especially important to the town, as humans transported their inventions and medicines, selling and trading to other people down river and beyond the North Sea. They also had floating hotels called river cruise ships, and humans of all ages loved to float up and down the river on them. It allowed visitors to see several countries' magnificent castles built on the hillsides along the river.

People could go horseback riding, ziplining, kayaking, canoeing, and explore castles. After their day's excursions, they would return to the same floating hotel and move along. Quite clever, I thought. Basel was not only a wonderful place to live but a profitable one as well.

As I thought of the wonderful country, the lump in my throat appeared again, and my heart ached for someone to care for.

I could live anywhere. I had no limits. A cockatrice is able to understand every language, but I chose Basel because of its interesting humans. Several were inventors, mathematic geniuses, and musicians. I thought it was one of the coolest places I had ever seen, but the town got dull once I became invisible.

I had often wondered if I gave up looking and failed, would I disappear like the others? For the past few years before, CGPs had been vanishing. I often wondered what my brothers and sisters were doing. I hadn't seen them in so long! I hoped they hadn't vanished too. I hadn't left to see my family because I thought I might miss an opportunity. I thought I would wait at least another day. I could wait a little longer.

"A job isn't a job at all, if you have fun and love it."

I'd often heard this, but my feathers burned red from the madness I felt inside. I cried outraged tears, and that's why I counted. My feet had grown tired of the cathedral roof, pacing back and forth for days, months, and years.

Being a CGP was the best job, and I was good at it! I'd looked after my little guardian children with pride. It was what I was born to do! I'd noticed how some of the other CGPs had simply looked after their human child, and they'd only stepped in when they were in danger.

Not me. I became much more to them—a friend and playmate—and I was rewarded with treats! How I missed those days.

In training, we had been taught that it was an instinct, and we would simply know when our guardian children would no longer need us. We would then leave them, vanishing from their minds, as if we had only been a foggy dream that faded in the midst of morning light. And the next one would then be right around the corner—really. I'd never had to go search for one. We had never been told what to do in that case. They would typically find us, so for that reason, I continued to sit and wait.

Some of my favorite guardian children have been the ones who had access to chocolate. I had a weakness for chocolate. I felt bad for those children I watched who had diabetes, but I would share the amount they could have and eat the rest, thus saving their lives at the same time. Around chocolate, my knees went weak, my tummy grumbled, my body shook, my feathers went askew, my feet started to dance, and the worst thing of all, I started to drool at the sight and smell of it.

About 420 years ago, a chocolate drink was brought to Europe. It was worth its weight in gold. The rich and powerful humans drank it at social gatherings to impress their friends and fellow townsmen. Prince and princesses, queens and kings, and rulers and emperors all had fountains of flowing warm chocolate that they drank. They would drink it in small little fancy cups that looked like a grandmother's china tea set, but a bit smaller.

In the 1600s, I remembered tucking my guardian child safely in bed before fluttering out among the adults and taking sips of their cocoa drinks. No one could see me, so it wasn't like I was going to get caught—however, there were some fights that broke out.

Several years later, chocolate became more than a socialite's drink. It had become common, and everyone could buy it. I was then able to sneak chocolate more often.

One important lesson I learned was to never, *never*, take the hidden dark chocolate from your guardian child's mother's bedside dresser. Everyone got in trouble when I took Mama's cocoa stash. Look both ways before crossing that danger bridge! Those are stories; they are my memories I think of while waiting for life to begin again.

Sitting on a balcony perched above the grand entrance of the cathedral of Basler Münster were three flags blowing in the breeze. One flag cracked like a whip, which startled me back to where I was, still waiting!

Tick, tock, tick, tock.

I listened to the steady pulse of the clock above me, and on the exterior of the building on the other side of me was the sundial clock. Both seemed to move slowly, as if they didn't work. Those long days of being unneeded and unseen seemed to crawl even slower than the turtle sunning down by the river bed.

That day, I was time watching, waiting to follow a small group of chocolatiers led by my personal favorite, a tour guide named Stephanie. She owned her own business called Xocotour—my translation of Xocotour is 'kiss of a chocolate tour.' I'd waited for days until I could smell Stephanie's perfume, her cocoa milk, and the chocolate treats and raw cacao beans she always had tucked away in her small carry bag. The other guides never carried one of those magical stuffed bags. I could sometimes smell the bag before she walked up the hill.

Throughout the tour, she was like a magician. She endlessly pulled things out of her little bag, which was filled with the best smelling cocoa from Switzerland. Excuse my drool, but it always happens at the thought of chocolate. I continued to look for Stephanie. She hadn't been here in days, but she had to come soon. I was in desperate need of chocolate.

Even though Stephanie couldn't see me as an adult, I was sure as a young girl she was a guardian child. She must have had a faerie-godparent or even a cockatrice CGP like myself. She had to have had a CGP that loved her, because of the love she had in her heart. During every tour, she would randomly place a piece of cocoa on the ledge of the gazebo, and I would fly over in a flash to snatch it up. Thinking back, I wondered why she did that?

Anyway, I know she wasn't from Basel. She

spoke at least four languages fluently, which made it difficult for me to know exactly where she was from. Either way, I could tell she had a wonderful soul, which meant that she was kind, honest, caring, and a zealous person. She was passionate about life and loved all creatures. And during the chocolate tours, she showed her compassion in the way she told her stories, sharing the history of the town and cocoa with those who wanted to learn.

CHAPTER FOUR

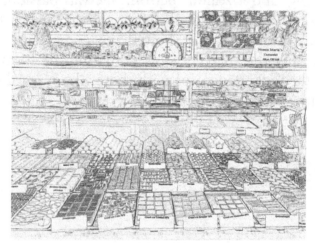

Brody

I T WAS OUR FIRST FULL day in Switzerland, and I think we slept for twelve hours that night. We had adjoining rooms with Mom and Dad. Being the middle child, I had to share a bed with Bryant if there were only two beds and a rollaway bed wasn't available. Once he fell asleep, he always tried to cuddle, and I had to push him away. Thank goodness I eventually found that putting a pillow between us helped. I love having a little brother, but sometimes it's a pain.

Bryant and I were the first to wake up and

were ready for the day to begin. That day, we would be taking a Swiss chocolate walking tour. The brochure said we would walk around Basel, tasting homemade chocolate from chocolatiers whose families had been making chocolate for hundreds of years.

We would ride the tramway back down the hill to the Mittlere Brücke stop, walk up a hill to Münsterplatz—the plaza where the Basel Minster Cathedral was located—and meet our chocolate tour guide. I couldn't wait for the three hours of walking and eating nothing but chocolate.

After tying my shoes, I packed both Bryant's and my day packs with our water bottles, swim suits, and travel towels. All we had to do was eat breakfast, and we were good to go. The next thing I needed to do was figure out how to wake everyone up and not let them realize it was me. I knew running water might work, or I could make coffee if I figured out how to work the coffee maker. The smell alone would wake everyone up.

Bryant must have read my mind. He went into Mom and Dad's room and turned on the television, looking for cartoons with the volume really loud. Even though it was in German, he sat on the foot of Mom and Dad's bed and loudly translated what he thought was being said for everyone. Mom woke Bowen, and he jumped in the shower. I hoped he would take a fast shower because I was hungry.

Mom and Dad eventually rushed us out of

our rooms and down the hall, and the five of us squeezed in the tiny European elevator.

Bryant asked, "Why are the elevators so small in Switzerland?"

"The people here don't eat all of your mom's good cooking," Dad replied.

Mom playfully jabbed Dad in the ribs and altered his response. "I think it's because they like to walk up and down the stairs. Elevators are for tourists and people with heavy luggage. Americans carry half their closet with them when they travel, and we need an elevator to get us and our huge bags to our rooms." Mom shook her head and giggled, and it made me wonder if that was the real reason.

We had a huge selection of food to choose from at the hotel's restaurant buffet, but because of time, we had to choose our food quickly and make our way to the tramway. No one wanted to miss the chocolate tour!

CHAPTER FIVE

Cody

PERCHED UP ABOVE THE MAIN door of the cathedral, I was losing patience with every passing day. My wings fluttered on their own, and my feathers were askew. My thoughts were unpredictable, and my mind went wild.

"The cure—I need chocolate! *Wait!* What is that I smell?"

A hint of delight tingled and tickled from my toes to my wings and nose. My body seemed to flutter about like a butterfly. I breathed deeply. My tail with its heart-shaped end pulsed with anticipation.

"It's her—Stephanie!"

I got a better look from the top of a flagpole on the balcony ledge. I loved watching her walk up the steep hill, taking the cobblestone roads that I had so many times.

Stephanie appeared in front of the cathedral in Münsterplatz with her red umbrella raised above her head, trying to hide from the bright ball of fire in the sky that humans called the sun. As she looked around the courtyard, a small group gathered around her.

She said, "*Guten morgen* (goo-ten morgen)." She spoke in German because that's what more than fifty percent of the people in Switzerland spoke. She then repeated the meaning in English, "Good morning." She introduced herself to the visitors, and after introductions were over, she began the tour.

Stephanie pointed to the Basler Münster's Gothic cathedral, and it looked as if she pointed to me.

I flew off the pole and back onto the railing of the balcony as if to hide from the people.

Stephanie explained that Saint Henry the Exuberant—the holy emperor—and his wife, Kunigunde, had been a huge reason for building the cathedral. Years later, it was dedicated to them. They wanted it to sit on this steeply sloping hill, so the building would sit above the Rhine River in the same location where the Roman fort had sat guarding the area. Stephanie pointed to the different colors of the bricks on the front of the cathedral, explaining that after the great earthquake in 1356, most of the original building had been destroyed.

As if I hadn't seen the front of the cathedral a billion times, I hopped back onto one of the ends of the flagpoles to get a better look at the bricks.

Stephanie continued, "The earthquake devastated the five towers and the choir lofts and various vaults inside. The Münster basically collapsed, and the process of rebuilding took place in several steps, spanning several hundred years."

She must have captivated her audience because the family of five, including the three young children, were listening to Stephanie's every word.

Continuing her story, she said, "It is much smaller now than the original building, and the brick's colors on the front don't match, but the building is unique for several reasons. One very important reason is that it shows not only the

Gothic style but the original Romanesque red sandstone architecture as well."

All three boys hung on every word, looking at the cathedral like they saw the ghosts of those long-dead people alive and walking around.

Walking near the cathedral, a little girl and her father caught the eye of the oldest of the three boys in Stephanie's group. When I leaned over to take another look at the young girl, the flagpole disappeared from under my feet, heading straight toward the girl's head. Reacting on instinct, I flew downward and thrust the flagpole, pushing it away from the girl and her father. The flagpole nearly hit both of them.

In unison, everyone around the cathedral sucked in air. When they noticed the father and daughter were safe, they let the air out of their lungs in relief.

Stephanie swooped toward the girl and her father, making sure they were all right. With help, Stephanie carried the flagpole inside the building.

My feathers ruffled, my dragon tail shook. It seems my reflexes worked, but I was more impressed by how Stephanie had leapt into action to help a stranger in need. When Stephanie came back outside, the little girl and her father were gone. Stephanie apologized to her group and decided to move onward.

I felt my feathers flush and turn a bright red. My rooster feet were heavy and curled tightly, gripping the railing once more. Was that my fault? If so, I could have caused a human child to be injured owing to my clumsiness. I could have flown, hovering, to see the wall, but instead I was perched on the pole. When I leaned out, I probably knocked it from its holder.

Maybe I shouldn't follow Stephanie. I didn't feel I deserved chocolate that day.

Chocolate... Well, maybe chocolate always has brought me luck. Hmmm.

I watched as the group walked away but couldn't resist the urge to follow.

Stephanie led her group down a narrow cobblestone street called Augustinergasse. They stopped at a water fountain, and Stephanie continued her dialog, sharing the history of Basel.

I fluttered up and landed on top of the larger-than-life-sized statue of a cockatrice. This statue was made in a rather mean fighting stance, and it reminded me a lot of one of my older brothers. He was a grumpy cockatrice, especially in the morning hours. We nicknamed him Dragon-child when we were younger.

The funny thing was, Dragon-child was one of the best CGPs of our kind. I envied him for that. I wondered how his retirement was going; he must have retired, because he had disappeared.

"This water is safe for anyone to drink," Stephanie added as she continued the tour.

I was not sure why this statue of Dragon-child didn't scare people away from filling their water containers. If humans were convinced that we were such beasts, they should all have run and hidden. Humans were so confusing.

My favorite part of Stephanie's tour came. She told the group more about the fabulous mythological creature, the cockatrice.

She said fabulous, I knew I liked her!

"A cockatrice, whose existence has not or cannot be proved…" Stephanie continued.

I jumped up and down, not convincing anyone. *I am real! I am here!*

But no one could see or hear me cry, so I continued to sit and listen to Stephanie's soothing voice continue, "A cockatrice was first referenced in Pliny's *Natural History*, a book about the whole of the natural world. Pliny was a Roman author and naval commander. He died in 79 AD, but his books were the largest collection to have survived from the Roman empire to modern times."

Stephanie finished speaking, and everyone turned to continue their walking tour down the small cobblestone road.

Stephanie's remarks about Pliny's books had gained the attention of the middle-sized child, named Brody. She continued, "It's amazing that thirty-seven of Pliny's books could have survived that many years. Not only did they survive the harsh Roman era but emperor takeovers and the hundreds, even thousands, of battles and wars. The Romans knew how important the first sets of the encyclopedia-type books were going to be. Well, these were intelligent people who had thrones (toilets) and plumbing in their homes. The ancient Greek Minoan civilization was the first to use underground clay pipes for sewer and water supply inside their homes, and that was more than 1,000 years before Christ (BC) or before the common era (BCE). If they invented indoor plumbing so long ago, the Romans must have known to keep Pliny's books safe." Stephanie ended her story and guided the group to the 'Garten of der Alten Universität.'

As everyone turned toward the steep steps to the garden, I dashed to the handrail. Balancing the rail between my rooster legs, I leaned back on my dragonlike tail and slid down the steep handrail to the end, tumbled to the ground, and tossed about like a fumbled football. I came to a stop and shook it off. That was the best part of the tour, well, after Stephanie and chocolate, of course.

I heard the middle boy named Brody turn to his mom and ask if he could slide down the handrail. She said it was too steep and he would get hurt. How would he get such an idea? A human would fall to his death sliding down this railing.

Everyone arrived at the gazebo and took a seat. I sat on the railing where I could watch Stephanie. She opened her magic bag, and my feet started dancing as she pulled out *cacao* seeds, handing one to everyone and placing one on the railing. They cautiously ate them, and I quickly snatched the one off the railing for myself. She pulled out five cocoa drinks, one for everyone in the group.

Isn't it wonderful!

I stuck my nose in the air and took in the aroma. If only I could have just one sip. The view from the gazebo overlooked the Rhine River, and as the group sipped on cocoa and watched the river, Stephanie told the history of the cacao plant.

She said, "The real way to say cocoa isn't the funny way you say it in English. It's pronounced 'cah-cow'."

Everyone repeated it, even though she didn't ask them, but every group seemed to do the same thing automatically. My whole body shook as I tried to stop myself from laughing.

Stephanie smiled, listening to the human parrots, and continued with her story of the history of the cacao plant as I drooled profusely once more. "The cacao trees are native to West Africa and Central America, but as far back as the 1600s and 1500s BC, the Mokaya tribes domesticated the bean. This was more than 3,500 years ago. They created a ritual beverage with cacao beans, water, vanilla beans, and chili spices, along with a dash or two of other spices."

As they all listened and watched the river, I tiptoed around, inspecting how much cocoa drink each one of them had left in their bottles. When the dad put his bottle on the ground, I slurped the last little drop of cocoa from it, hoping someone else would put theirs down.

Stephanie said, "The Olmecs and the Mayas shared these drinks only in betrothal and marriage ceremonies. The Aztecs believed that cacao seeds were the gift of Quetzalcoatl, the god of wisdom."

At that moment, Brody put his bottle down between his feet. He had at least a few sips left in the bottle, and I carefully snuck over and sipped the remaining cocoa.

"The cacao seeds were so valuable they were used as currency," Stephanie continued. "On the Yucatan peninsula where the Maya Indians were around 600 AD, they called it the *food of the gods*."

I nodded, agreeing with the fact that cacao was the *food of the gods*. I noticed the middle boy doing the same, nodding his head in agreement.

The middle boy, Brody, took the information in like a computer processor, quickly and efficiently. Brody had realized one thing—one important thing. We were nowhere near Central America or West Africa. When, why, and how did the cacao seeds get to Switzerland?

Then I realized I could "hear" most of the American boys' thoughts. Strange. I could normally only hear my guardian child's thoughts. I could have been assuming that's what he was thinking. Ya, that was it!

Stephanie, while collecting the empty jars of cocoa drink, concluded her cacao lesson, saying, "A famous Spanish explorer, Conquistador Don Hernán Cortés, discovered the bean while exploring Central America. He brought the bean back to Spain in 1528 because he thought it would be a product of value."

I listened to Stephanie but started to watch the boys—especially the one named Brody—carefully. Stephanie signaled for the group to follow her as she walked away from the gazebo. Brody's eyes seem fixated on Stephanie and his attention on her stories, but they would then wander in my direction before dashing back toward Stephanie.

"It took more than 100 years before it reached and was traded all over Europe," Stephanie added. "At first it was only used as a social drink for rich and powerful people, but now look how far it has evolved. We can buy it at every corner store." Stephanie pointed to the Confiserie Bachmann. "This is one of the oldest family-owned chocolate makers in Basel."

The store's owners had invited Stephanie and her groups to go upstairs into the kitchen, where they made the tasty treats that lined the display cases in the front store. It smelled heavenly to everyone, at least those who liked chocolate.

Typically, I didn't like going inside of the Confiserie Bachmann. Once when I'd followed her group upstairs to the kitchen, my wings created a little breeze and caused quite the stir. Then I missed the door and had to turn the knob with my roosterlike feet, but the door was much larger than one at a house. I could have easily broken the door or knocked it down, but I didn't want Stephanie to be blamed for the damage, and it took me a while to find a window to make my escape. So, it was easier for me to wait outside. But on this particular tour, nothing seemed to keep me away.

I watched as Brody walked into the kitchen. He looked as if he was searching for something. As Stephanie showed them the huge pots of chocolate and the freezer full of treats, Brody looked and looked again. He had a way of inspecting things, measuring in his head and processing how equipment worked and how it was used. I wondered if this was simply a Brody thing, the mind of an engineer, or if he were looking for me.

CHAPTER SIX

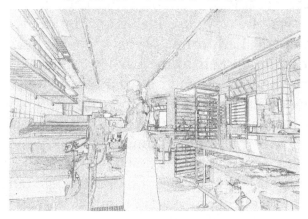

Brody

OUR NEXT STOP WAS A couple blocks up the street. As we entered the building with a sign saying Confiserie Schiesser - seit 1870, I noticed the 'since 1870' sign. We went up the stairs to a private dining area where we sat and tasted 100 percent cacao.

"The difference between cocoa and cacao is that cacao is raw. Cacao that has been toasted at high temperatures becomes cocoa, an ingredient in chocolate—the chocolate most kids enjoy, and it is much cheaper than cacao," Stephanie explained. "Cacao 100 percent is made by cold-pressing an unroasted cacao bean. This keeps the enzymes in the cacao and removes the fat. The fat is also known as the cacao butter. This is the purest form of chocolate, and it's actually good for you."

I looked at Bowen and Bryant. Their eyes grew large, and I wanted a pound of this for dinner!

Stephanie smiled. "It has the highest form of antioxidants in foods and has a high number of flavonoids, which is a plant and fungus."

"Gross," I said out loud. "A fungus?"

Stephanie nodded and continued, "It is high in protein, fiber, magnesium, and iron. You should not have more than six teaspoons a day."

"Aww, bummer," Bowen said.

Stephanie broke off a tiny piece of the 100 percent cacao bar and gave everyone a taste. I couldn't tell you how disappointed I was when she only handed me a small little sliver of cacao and placed one in the hand of each of us.

Stephanie quickly added, "Make sure you glide the cacao around with your tongue to feel the texture of the cacao. The smoother it is, the better the quality."

When I saw Bowen pop the whole sliver into his mouth, Bryant and I followed suit. It didn't take more than a moment to notice that this cacao wasn't anything like our favorite milk chocolate.

I couldn't help the gag-sensation I was having, which made Bryant run to Mom with tears in his eyes. Cacao slid out of his open mouth like a river of mud and saliva. Bowen's lips and mine became brown, and a thick ooze seeped from our lips. We couldn't keep it inside our mouths. Bryant gagged as Mom scrambled for a napkin. Bowen and I both froze, afraid of throwing up.

We searched for a napkin and spit it out. It was disgusting, and worse, it didn't leave our mouths willingly. It stuck to every tooth and crevasse. Our water bottles didn't hold enough water to get relief, so copying Bowen, I took my napkin and scrubbed my tongue.

Stephanie giggled and slipped all of us a piece of milk chocolate. We were skeptical but took her offering. We glanced at Mom for approval. All three of us were worried it would be the same bitter stuff we had just scrubbed out of our mouths. With a nod from Mom, we popped the chocolate in our mouths and were very pleased with the milk chocolate flavor relieving our taste buds from the dark fungus that had the texture of slime.

Soon after, we continued our tour at the Walk of Fame. Famous people from Basel had their names inscribed on nameplates that were scattered down the road. It reminded me of Hollywood Boulevard in California, where the famous people had their names and stars down the sidewalk. We stopped to take a picture with Roger Federer's nameplate.

With eyebrows raised, Dad said, "Roger Federer is one of the top ten men's tennis players in the world and has been since 2002. I didn't realize he was born in Basel."

I looked quickly for Edwin Fischer. He was a famous piano arranger born in Basel, but I didn't have any luck finding his nameplate before we had to make our way to the next chocolate shop. My piano teacher would have been impressed if I had come home with a photograph of Edwin Fischer's nameplate, especially since she had recently told me about him.

As we continued our walk up the small little cobblestone street, we saw a restaurant called Barfi's.

No way!

Bowen started to make barfing sounds, saying, "Baaarrrrffffi's!"

We laughed so hard and couldn't stop giggling about it for the next two blocks. We continued begging Mom and Dad to let us eat dinner at Barfi's. We arrived at another cockatrice fountain and stopped to refill our water bottles. We took turns collecting the water from the cockatrice's mouth.

I decided to brave it and asked Mom, "Why are there two cockatrices?"

Mom answered, "There are several water fountains with the cockatrice statues."

I was not sure she understood the question, but I didn't bother trying to explain what I meant. I asked Dad, but he wasn't much help either. Adults could be so frustrating. The only thing that made sense was the cacao had started to get to me. Maybe I was tired.

Ya, that's it. I have jet leg!

I honestly thought I saw a real eight-inch cockatrice perched on top of the statue's arched neck. But that couldn't be right. They were mythological, meaning—fake! There must have been a bird in Basel that looked a lot like the statue or something. The bird—or cockatrice—kept showing up at almost every stop we made on the tour, almost as though Stephanie had a pet cockatrice, and he was following her.

The cockatrice landed on the ground near my feet. As I walked, I had to step around the cockatrice, and we looked into each other's eyes. I knew then he wasn't real. A cockatrice in mythological terms could kill with a single glance, and only a weasel was immune to their deadly stare! I couldn't remember what other powers they had.

"Bowen, what other powers does a cockatrice have?" I asked.

"I think they have deadly breath, and they will turn you to stone with a glance," Bowen answered.

We walked into the next chocolate store, and the little eight-inch cockatrice perched himself on one of the display shelves. I tried my hardest not to look into his eyes again, but he stared at me every time I glanced his way.

Stephanie handed everyone a small square piece of pink cacao. This was a double warning for all of us. Pink chocolate couldn't taste good. Very cautious of eating cacao at that point, we watched Dad take his first bite. We knew he hadn't enjoyed the dark 100 percent cacao either, so Dad would be a safe judge regarding the pink cacao's taste.

Dad twirled the pink chocolate around in his mouth, then swallowed and said, "Tasty."

We took this as approval and put the pink cacao in our mouths. Bowen wasn't impressed, but Bryant's eyes lit up with pleasure.

Smiling, Stephanie told the shortened story of how the ruby chocolate had been made with unfermented ruby cacao beans. "These ruby beans come from Brazil, and it is a natural color. This ruby chocolate treat is a mixture of the ruby cacao and its fat, the ruby cacao butter. Ruby chocolate was developed in 2004. It was then introduced to Europe and Japan in 2017, Canada in 2019, and isn't sold in the United States. These unfermented beans are what gives the ruby chocolate a sweet, yet sour taste."

I personally thought it tasted like white and milk chocolate mixed with a little bit of raspberries. It was wonderful, so I asked Mom and Dad to buy some. I wanted at least twelve bars—they were small bars.

We walked back to the Münsterplatz without my dozen ruby chocolate bars. They had been sold out. We made our way down another set of steep steps to the river, where we boarded the

Münster-Fahre "LEU," a motorless boat that was tethered to a long line across the river. We rode in the Leu all the way to the other side of the Rhine's river bank.

Bowen instantly started making little jokes about the Leu. "You better not go loo on the leu, either way we would lose."

Any potty joke was funny to him. As the leu drifted across the river, something in the water splashed, and several people got wet. Everyone yelped and pointed, asking one another if they saw the fish jump.

I turned to my parents and said, "It wasn't a fish, it was a cockatrice."

Both my parents giggled.

"You must have had too much chocolate," my Mom commented.

Oh, parents!

That was embarrassing. I sat, silently angry at the remark, but my statement did sound crazy.

We left the Leu at the dock and walked down the river walk, where we came across a grand piano. It sat on the sidewalk outside of an apartment building. Stephanie said she had never seen this piano before, but she knew a family had been moving out. Maybe they had left it there until someone could come move it.

The piano called to me, and I quietly slid onto the bench seat and began to play. Stephanie paused and looked at me as if to move us along, but then she listened to a few measures and allowed me to finish. I was so deeply involved in playing, I didn't notice the small pile of Swiss francs starting to pile up on the baby grand piano.

As people walked past, they paused to listen and leave me tip money, but I didn't notice until I was finished. I only played a part of a Minuet Suite by J. S. Bach and slid right into Mozart's Sonata Number 16 in C. I then looked up to notice several strangers standing around and watching. I slowly stood, and everyone clapped. I had no idea what to do.

Should I bow or what?

My face flushed, and I wished I was invisible. Suddenly, I saw the cockatrice land on the piano, and he pointed to the loot. I gave a glance toward Mom and Dad, and they nodded in agreement for me to take the money. They walked away, following Stephanie into a little coffee shop bookstore where she ended the tour. I gave Stephanie my tip money and thanked her for the tour. Mom and Dad smiled at me and said that I had a kind heart.

If my heart was kind, it wouldn't be a heart with issues.

As we walked out the coffee shop door, Stephanie said, "*Danke* (dunk-ah), *auf wiedersehen* (owf-vee-da-zane)."

We all replied thank you and said goodbye back to Stephanie.

I noticed the cockatrice following us into and

out of Stephanie's store and asked, "Bryant, do you see that little bird thing following us?"

Bryant nodded in reply.

I wondered if Bryant had heard me correctly as we continued walking down the street.

CHAPTER SEVEN

Cody

EVEN THOUGH I WASN'T CONVINCED Brody could see me, I continued shadowing the American family. There was something about those kids, and I wanted to understand more. I had never monitored other tourists or groups besides the Xocotour tours, but I was curious about that American family. Could he see me, and if so, why? Because they were American? It didn't work like that, did it? Plus, they seemed perfect, inside and out.

As the family walked the one-lane streets, they talked and pointed at the buildings, windows, stores, apartment-type buildings, and even plants and flowers. They threw questions at their parents, wondering why the shops weren't open, why the buildings looked so different than at home, and why they had never seen that plant or bird before. When they reached the busy street—the main street headed toward the Rhine River—I followed them toward the Mittlere Brücke bridge.

When they reached the small cafe with outside tables, they sat and ordered a couple sandwiches to share. Their mom and dad agreed that they could float the river after lunch. They changed into their swimsuits, and their dad purchased everyone colorful Wickelfisch. These were dry bags that were made in Basel, shaped like fish to keep clothes, towels, and personal items dry while floating down the river.

They filled their Wickelfisch bags and held onto the rope, and one by one, the whole family jumped into the water. I decided to make a splash like they did and jumped, landing a belly flop right beside Bryant, the youngest of the three boys. He began to laugh so hard it impaired his swimming a little, so I secured his Wickelfisch closer to him as he swam.

Baffled, I wondered why he was laughing. Did I miss something? Did he see me too? Never in all my CGP life had two kids from the same family been able to see me, but I was not convinced either had actually seen me; however, I could hear them both think, and that's the first thing on a CGP's checklist when we arrived at our new guardian child's location. The two boys' thoughts are mixed—almost scrambled together—making it complicated. I couldn't figure out who was thinking what. It confused me.

Bowen, the oldest boy, swam swiftly past Brody while holding the end of his Wickelfisch rope, his bag following behind. I swam underneath Brody and popped out of the water onto Bowen's bag. Brody's eyes widened as he stared at me. This eye-to-eye contact caught me off guard, and with a tug of the rope from Bowen, I slipped and fell back into the cold river.

Brody giggled and looked at his brothers to see if they saw me. No one else reacted, nor did they seem to see me perched on top of Brody's bag. I shook the water from my feathered head. As we floated under the Mittlere Brücke bridge, the family kicked toward the riverbank because the water flow pushed people toward the center of the river. The water moved quickly, so the boys' dad and mom began to plan how they would all get out at the same time, at least near the same location.

The three boys were very strong swimmers for their ages, but their parents didn't want to underestimate the power of the current. Their dad was closest to Bryant, so he swiftly grabbed the side of the river walk wall, tossing Bryant onto the slick edge of the platform where they had chosen to exit. Bowen followed their mom out, landing only feet away from the others. Brody grabbed the wall at the same time as Bowen, but Brody lost grip of his bag's rope. He let go of the wall and swam for the bag.

As Brody lost the string of his Wickelfisch, the river's turbulence swiftly took over. Brody's strength was no match for this river, and a rush of panic flushed over him. I was at his side and handed him the rope, guiding him back toward the river wall.

When Brody was safely at the wall, he whispered, "Thank you."

Brody saw me!

Completely dumbfounded, I didn't know what else to do, so I flew away back to the streets and cobblestones to count.

"One, two, three…"

Cobblestones placed together with such care hundreds of years ago.

"Four, five, six…"

With each small stride.

"Seven, eight, nine…" …

"I am Cody the Cockatrice of Basel, Switzerland! Why can an American boy see me?"

I wandered around the cobblestone streets and found myself in front of the Radisson Blu Hotel. How could this be? An American boy believed in me? He and his family are tourists, and they would be leaving soon. I should have been dancing in the streets, shouting on rooftops. This boy apparently needed me, plus he believed! I'd waited so long, but what would I do?

"Ten, eleven, twelve…"

I got it! I knew what to do! I would wait for Brody to exit the hotel.

From twilight to dawn, I watched as the sky changed to various colors of blue through the soft city lights. Walking, sitting, and even fluttering about in circles, I paced. I waited, watching the front doors swing open and softly shut again. I stared at the name of the hotel, which read Rad Blu Hotel. Maybe Brody needed me while he visited Basel. He had needed me today.

That's it! I should watch him while he's in Basel.

CHAPTER EIGHT

Brody

AFTER AN EARLY DINNER AT Barfi's—where the food kind of matched the name, I hated to say—we got back to the hotel, showered, and played games. Mom and Dad went downstairs to check us in for the river cruise.

My favorite chocolate was the ruby chocolate, but Mom and Dad had only found one bar left for sale. They said we would find more in Köln, Germany—or, as Americans spelled it, Cologne. Stephanie had told us that it was a new creation and had been added as one of the chocolate flavors: dark, white, milk, and ruby. I would not be able to live on cacao (cah – cow) alone, but it was the *food of the gods,* and it was worth buying as much as we could. Right!

"Hey, Bryant? You know the little…well, the little birdlike creature we saw today? Was it real?" I whispered to him in the bathroom.

Bryant's eyes spoke volumes, but he scrunched his shoulders toward his ears and said, "I don't know. He looks like one of those statues we got our water from, but that's a cockatrice, and they are supposed to be deadly and not real. The real one looks cute, not mean."

"I know, right! But a cockatrice's deadly weapon is its stare. A glance into someone's eyes should turn them to stone, and I looked into his eyes a couple times today, and here I am!" I replied. "Do you think Bowen saw him?"

At that moment, Bowen walked into the room. Bryant dove into his game, and I turned mine off to grab a book. I stared at the words written on the pages, but I couldn't read a word.

Bowen seemed to be extra quiet that night, and he hadn't picked on either one of us once. Typically, if Mom and Dad left us for too long, we would have been in the midst of a pillow fight or some argument, or at least playing a game together. That night, I wasn't the only one thinking about something else. I put the book back in my backpack and lay down on the bed, staring at the ceiling.

Bowen sat next to me. "I think I might be getting sick or something."

"What?" I replied.

"Well, I've been seeing something all day, and it's like my imagination is going wild on me. I don't know how to explain it. My mind is playing tricks on me. I saw a mythological creature today." Bowen sounded a little freaked out.

I looked toward Bryant. He lifted his head from his game and nodded.

"Bowen, I think I—or we—know what you are talking about."

Bowen looked at me, then over to Bryant. "You both saw it too?" Bowen asked.

Bryant nodded.

"What the heck? What is it? Who else can see it?" Bowen asked in one swift breath.

"Those are good questions, but we don't know." I answered, wondering if we would ever see it again.

"Guys," Bowen said firmly, "we can never—ever—never tell anyone about this! Do you hear me?"

Bryant and I nodded, and we didn't wait for Mom and Dad to put us to bed. Even with the lights off, I could tell that Bryant and Bowen were staring at the ceiling too.

Cutting the silence, Bowen said, "It had to be

a bird, some kind of bird from Switzerland. We just haven't seen it before."

The only thing we heard after that was our breathing.

CHAPTER NINE

Cody

I T WAS MORNING. I WAITED for the American family to come out for their next day's adventure. I am not convinced I'm Brody's CGP because I can't hear him. I hear garbled babble—a mix of words. It's not clear. I should have heard his thoughts from out here if he were my guardian child.

Two large luxury buses parked, obscuring my

view. I fluttered around, quickly finding a new spot. Luckily, I didn't look away because in the corner of my eye, I saw Brody and his family boarding one of the white buses sitting outside.

A bus. Why not the tramway?

I followed the bus around the city, toward Basel's north docks on the Rhine River. The buses arrived at the river cruise ship docks.

"They must be taking a cruise."

Curiously, I watched as a dozen tourists unloaded from the bus. Finally, Brody's family made their way off and onto the gangplank. The floating hotel seemed to be awaiting their arrival. The river ship's name was *Ama Kristina*, and she was one of the Once Upon the Rhine River cruise ships.

I perched on the railing, wondering what I should do next as I watched Brody and his family waiting on the gangplank. As the family inched forward to go aboard, Brody turned toward me. He waved his hand, concealing the gesture from his family. I cocked my head from side to side like a puppy and almost whimpered.

Oh, my goodness, it's true, he sees me.

My insides tightened. I heard him think! I felt paralyzed like one of the bronzed cockatrice statues overlooking the water fountains.

The little boy from America could see me! I could hear him! That day, I was not-so-invisible Cody the Cockatrice! In all my years of CGP training, it meant that I was Brody's CGP. Rules were rules, but I quivered at the thought.

The dilemma of my coming from Basel and Brody living in America was never addressed in any of my CGP classes. We would find children to watch from our town, and we stayed with them. We didn't find a child from another country and move. It didn't happen.

Maybe it did, I don't know.

I jumped down and onto the Riverwalk. There were no cobblestones to count, but I started to walk anyway. I peeked over my shoulder and noticed Brody watching me walk back and forth several times. My head was lowered like I was looking for something on the ground. I started to drag my chicken toes across the pavement.

I don't know what to do!

CHAPTER TEN

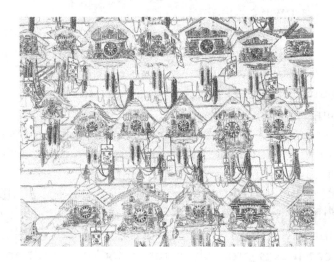

Brody

THE ADVENTURE GUIDES WELCOMED us aboard the *Ama Kristina*, introducing themselves as songs played softly in the background. Two large, white-gloved hands sat on the front desk counter that read, WELCOME ABOARD. I became even more excited.

My brothers and I flung questions at Mom and Dad like bullets in a nerf gun war.

"Can we go explore?"

"Can we go to the top deck?"

"Can we go check out the ship?"

After failed attempts to lose our parents, we all checked out our new cabins. I quickly told Bowen and Bryant that I'd seen the cockatrice, and we agreed to try and go up on the top deck to at least wave goodbye.

In our room, our luggage waited for us, and we called dibs on beds and places for our belongings. Moments later, we hurried Mom and Dad out of their cabin door to explore the rest of the ship.

An area for games, snacks, and lounging was on the main deck. The top deck had a pool, a sitting area, lots of sun chairs, and shaded areas too. Bowen, Bryant, and I ran toward the side of the ship to see if we could find the little cockatrice, but he'd disappeared. Bowen tried to convince us that it was probably a funny-looking bird, and we'd simply seen several of them throughout the day. I knew better, but we had to leave it alone. We were about to leave Basel and the birdlike cockatrice.

We continued exploring the river ship, but it was time to head back down to the main deck and hit up the chocolate treats and cookies. Our adventure guides had planned a meet-and-greet as a group. Six stops, seven nights, several excursions, lots of food, and every one of the guides seemed happy—extraordinarily happy! As if this were the happiest place on earth.

I looked out the window to see if I could get

a last glance at my little friend the cockatrice, but he was nowhere to be seen. Well, it seemed that almost everyone was cheerful, but something was sad about leaving the creature. It's not as if... Well, we didn't even know his name.

Maybe Bowen was right. It wasn't real. Maybe it was just a strange bird that we kept seeing time after time. As the crowd clapped and the adventure guide's introduction ended, I slid some extra treats and cookies into a napkin and followed my family to the top deck. We watched Basel disappear off the ship's stern as the *Ama Kristina* made her way down the Rhine River.

We arrived in our rooms late after dinner and unpacked our bags. I remembered the cookies I had taken from the buffet, took the napkin out, and placed it on the nightstand beside my bed. We didn't talk about the cockatrice because I didn't want to sound like a crazy person. So, we played a game and then went to sleep.

Clang-clink, clink-thunk.

"I can't open the bathroom door!" Bryant yelled, waking Bowen and me from a deep sleep.

By the time I focused my eyes in the light of the early morning dawn, Bowen had jumped from his bed, grabbed Bryant by the hand, and led him in the opposite direction to the bathroom. Bryant had attempted to open the sliding door to the balcony when he yelled. He had either been sleepwalking, or he was just confused, and the balcony door was jammed. Thank goodness it wouldn't open.

I walked toward the balcony's sliding door, and it slid open easily. "Bowen, this door was unlocked. He could have walked off the ship," I stated. I turned around and noticed my cookies were gone. "Bryant, did you eat my cookies?" I asked, knowing he wouldn't admit to it if he did.

"No!" Bryant denied from inside the bathroom, just as I figured he would.

It was morning, so we dressed for the day, not realizing the ship's slight movement throughout the night had kept us in a deep sleep much longer than expected. Mom and Dad knocked on the door and led the way to the dining room, where we found out that we were docked in Strasbourg, France.

"We are in France! It's as if we are country-jumping!" Bryant said with a cheery glee.

Strasbourg bordered Germany, and Mom had planned two separate excursions. Mom and Bryant would go horseback riding with another small group from the ship. The horse farm was in France, located on one side of the Rhine River. Meanwhile, Dad, Bowen, and I would head to the other side of the river to go ziplining in Germany.

The heavenly smell of pancakes, bacon, sausage, and eggs guided us to the huge breakfast buffet.

"*Bonjour* (bohn-jor), are you ready for your *aventure* (ah-von-toor)?" greeted Calli, the adventure guide who would head to France with the horseback riders. She waited for an answer from Bryant and helped him with saying "*oui*" (we) or "*non*" (noh)."

Bryant giggled, shook his head and said, "*Oui*, yes!"

Jackson, our adventure guide to Germany, said, "*Guten morgen* (goo-ten mor-gen), and are you ready for your ziplining *abenteur* (ah-ben-the-yoor)?"

Bowen and I replied together, "*Ja* (yah), yes, we are!"

After we ate, Dad, Bowen, and I boarded the adventure bus with Jackson and about ten other adventure cruisers. Our first stop was the Black Forest Triberg waterfalls. The Black Forest, named because of its dark-colored pine trees, was the home of the Grimm fairy tales and cuckoo clocks.

Our hiking shoes were laced up, and we carried water bottles in hand as we entered the forest, an area that suddenly swallowed us in darkness. Walking into the Black Forest totally reminded me of the story of Hansel and Gretel. I suddenly realized how the Grimm brothers had come up with Hansel and Gretel—and their other stories—while living in this area. Darkness fell around us, and the smell of something musty and strange lingered in the air. People walked nearby, but they seemed to be fading off in a blur. I felt like the forest was swallowing me whole.

As the whole group climbed the steep walking

trail, I sucked the air in but had no sensation of air filling my lungs. The people around me fell off into the distance, fuzzy and blurry. Suddenly, I felt tired and wished I could lie down and sleep. Dad touched my shoulder and encouraged me to move onward, and I realized I was standing, not lying down. I told my feet to move, but the world spun quickly around me. I felt dizzy, and something like a giant sponge seemed to be lodged in my windpipe. I gasped for breath. It seemed like I had fallen into the water and was drowning.

When I woke from the fog, I was outside the forest and near the entrance gates, wondering how in the world I got there. Alone, I stood near a beautiful flower topiary, and I was gasping for breath. My lungs started to fill back with air, and my eyes filled with water. Then I began to sneeze—nonstop and uncontrollably.

Dad guided me to a bench, where he sat next to me. I didn't remember sitting down, but besides my sneezing, everything seemed all right. Beads of sweat rolled down my cheeks. We sat and waited for the group to return from the waterfalls. To get out of the sun and the heat, Dad took me inside one of the many stores that lined the little town.

Dad later said he asked me several questions, but I don't remember talking. The adventure group appeared from the forest, and Bowen went on and on about how cool it was. Jackson asked Dad all sorts of questions, but my head was still in a fog. Jackson asked a doctor who was traveling with us to just look at me and whether they needed to take me to the hospital, but the doctor said that I might have had an allergic reaction to something in the Black Forest.

Someone had given me some allergy medicine, and I felt much better. I followed Bowen and Dad into a cuckoo clock store. Thousands of handmade cuckoo clocks ticked, clinked, and chimed, and when the hour hand reached the top, music sounded. The melodies of the "Cuckoo Waltz," "Milla The Black Forest," and others like the "Wood Chopper" and "Lorelei" danced in the store. As soon as they ended their sweet chimes, the sounds of tick, clink, and cranking began again.

Each cuckoo had been hand-carved with amazing animals or birds. Some had people dancing and some working saws. Amazed by the details, I realized each told a story of its own. Bowen and I took it all in, eyeing each clock carefully, even though I felt sluggish and tired.

Bowen asked, "Did you see the cockatrice?"

"I did not, where is he?" I asked.

"I think he took you out of the forest," Bowen said, looking sincere.

"I thought Dad carried me out," I replied.

"Dad was with me until you went missing," Bowen said as he ran his finger along the cuckoo clock's roof.

We continued around the store. Both tiny

and huge cuckoos lined the walls, with so many detailed, moving parts. I thought of my Legos and wondered if it would be possible to make a cuckoo clock with them. My sneezes slowed, and my mind went adrift, as if it were in a boat floating through the fog. I didn't have the strength to ask Dad to buy me a cuckoo, but I was alert enough to see the huge price tags and know what the answer would be.

We met the group for lunch, and after we loaded back on the bus, we headed to another area of the Black Forest. Dad gave me another allergy pill to take, and I felt much better. My sneezing stopped, and I slept for the hour-long bus ride. When the bus came to a halt, we parked on the hillside on a very narrow one-lane road in the Hirschgrund Black Forest.

The group followed Jackson to a small shack, where they gathered to receive instructions for the zipline. Bowen and I put our harnesses and helmets on, then we started the trek up the mountain following Jackson, Dad, and the others.

We huffed up the incredibly steep mountain. I wondered if maybe I was having strange allergic reactions or travel fatigue, and Bowen and I both wished our little friend was still with us. The trek up the mountain was brutal, more so than anyone thought it would be.

Dad kept asking me if I was all right, and I told him I felt fine.

I wish everyone would stop asking me if I am

okay. Great, one more thing to add to my medical alert bracelet—Allergic to the Black Forest!

We finally reached the top zipline, where we climbed on top of the structure to reach the cables suspended between the trees. I drank almost all of my water and was thankful Dad had carried the backpack with our water up the mountain. One by one, we hooked our harness onto the pulley. Anticipation mounted as we listened to the instructor, then one by one, we waited to step off the platform. Way above the tree line, we stood, trusting these wires to hold us all as we zipped down to the next platform.

It was my turn, so I gripped the hoop and double-checked my harness. When I heard the word, I released and followed Dad down the zipline. Propelled by gravity and flying above the Black Forests' trees, rivers, and streams, I heard screams of delight and fear from the others echo off the mountain valley. From the top of one tree to the next platform, we were officially called Flying Zippers, the nickname that all zipliners earned. However, Bowen and I liked the nickname the Flying Fox much better as soon as we heard it.

We zipped along, laughing, hooting, and trying our best foxlike sounds. The trees were becoming denser the further down we zipped. Each platform became deeper and lower the farther we went.

As I zipped down the fifth line, my airway

tightened again, and I gasped for air. I couldn't yell, and if I did, everyone would only think that I was having a good time. I felt like I was underwater again, trying desperately to breathe. My throat closed tighter, I felt like someone was choking me, and my grip on the loop weakened. I suddenly felt sleepy when everything went dark.

A swift gust of wind brought me back from the darkness. Wind swirled around me, and air filled my lungs. Dad must have seen my distress because he caught me as I arrived at the platform structure. Bowen and the adventure guide, Jackson, were standing and waiting to hook up to the next cable but had waited because of me. Jackson and Dad agreed that I was allergic to something in the Black Forest, and here we were, surrounded by it.

Ziplining was the fastest way out. Dad handed me his bandana, and I covered my nose and mouth, wrapping it around my head like a cow-boy riding in a dust storm. I hesitated, shaking at the edge of the platform.

I heard a whisper in my ear. "The fear may not ever go away. You might have to do it afraid, but I am with you. Cody is with you."

Pulling the bandana up, I jumped. A fresh gust of air from above fanned down and around me. I was so thankful. I made it down with no problem. On the bus, I fell asleep, and when I woke, I looked around for my small friend but realized maybe I'd been dreaming.

"I think his name is Cody," I whispered to Bowen before I fell back to sleep on the bus.

Later, I walked onto the *Ama Kristina* as if I slogged through deep sludge. My legs felt heavy, and I couldn't wait to lie down in a bed.

When I walked into our room, I noticed that Jackson and the other adventure guides had left a box of macaron cookies for me in my cabin with a note wishing me a quick recovery. I'd never had macarons before, but they looked yummy. The brightly colored puffy sandwiches looked like pieces of art, if you asked me. The card said the cookie was introduced by an Italian chef in France for the queen, Catherine de Medici, in the Renaissance period.

Mom sat with me for a couple hours, I think. While I drifted in and out of sleep, she told me about her and Bryant's riding adventure in France. She later left for dinner, saying she would be back every few minutes or so to check on me, but by that time, I felt fine. I waited a minute after Mom shut the door before I opened the balcony door to go sit outside and eat my macaron cookies. I placed the opened box out on the table and slid back inside for a second to retrieve my water bottle. When I went back outside, the cookie box was empty. I looked around for birds or thought it was Bowen playing a trick on me, but I saw no one and thought maybe I was more out of it than I first thought, so I went back inside to sleep.

I slept through dinner and into the next morning. As I awoke, I had the feeling someone was watching me. I was a bit weirded out but not scared. I thought it would be a good idea to get some fresh air, so I slipped outside, trying not to wake Bryant and Bowen. I watched the sunrise, mesmerized as the dark blue faded and brilliant oranges and pinks brushed onto the canvas of the horizon beyond the city of Strasbourg. It was beautiful. I don't remember ever watching a sunrise, at least not one that memorable.

CHAPTER ELEVEN

Cody

I LOVED FRENCH MACARONS. NOT AS much as I loved chocolate, but they were so good. I had to hide from Brody, so I ate them on his parents' balcony, concealed by the divider and out of Brody's sight, of course. That was my dinner but after I snuck back into the cabin, I slept on

Brody's bed, hoping he wouldn't wake and see me. I was sound asleep when I heard Brody slide the door open and go outside to watch the sunrise. Quickly, I dashed away, hiding in a pile of dirty boy smells—the laundry pile. I was lucky I didn't sleep on the other side of his bed because he would have rolled out and mushed me.

I needed to speak with my siblings—any of them would do at that point! I didn't have time to speak with Clara the day before in the Black Forest, but I had been very thankful for her help with the wind creation she'd helped me make, getting fresh air to Brody when he was ziplining down the mountain. I should have stayed and asked, but I was worried about Brody.

The sun started to rise. The boys began waking, and the room was getting brighter. I was thankful the three boys had a heaping pile of laundry for me to hide in, but I wished it wasn't the dirty laundry. When the family rustled about during the morning, readying for the day, they dressed and were on their way to the dining room without seeing me.

They were welcomed to breakfast with several Guten Morgens from the adventure guides. People happily replied *danke* (dunk-ah) and *guten morgen* (goo-ten mor-gen) back. There was something very satisfying about hearing people trying to speak the native language, even though it was only to say thank you and good morning.

After breakfast, they all gathered with their groups. Brody's whole family followed Missy, the adventure guide from Missouri in America. Or do they say Missouri, United States? Well, anyway, Missy wore blue. Each guide wore a different color, and it represented the different excursions or buses they were going on.

Brody's family headed to Strasbourg for their adventure by way of Botorama Riverboat. Oh, I loved Botoramas! It was a small canal boat enclosed with glass sides and a roof top, enabling a fabulous view of the canals of Strasbourg, France. The sun shone, and most of the windows were open on that beautiful summer day. The fresh air seemed to agree with Brody, as he looked much better, smiling as he watched their boat go through the river's locks.

The lock lowered the boat down, much like an elevator, lowering or raising a boat into the next level of a river or channel. However, all three boys found themselves whispering to one another about how fun it would be to tube down the cascading water over the rocks. I finally started to realize why they needed a cockatrice.

The lock gate opened, and away the boat went, puttering down the next channel. It wound through the canals, past towers, and floated under beautiful brick arched bridges, nearing the Vauban Dam.

The Vauban Dam, also known as the Great

Lock, was built more than 300 years ago. I was there with my sister, Pia, when they finished building the Great Lock in 1690 for their celebrations.

The tour seemed to flow right by, and I had to get ahead of the tour group to find Pia. It had been about forty-five years since I had seen her. She was not going to be happy with me about that. I know, I know. I needed to go see my siblings more often. She would know I was there if I went to the Strasbourg Cathedral de Notre Dame. I wasn't committed to Brody, so leaving to find Pia wasn't against the CGP rules or anything. I left and flew around the area, to the cathedral, darting in and out of every corner and even up in the rafters, way above the people. Until there wasn't a place I hadn't looked.

At the Strasbourg Cathedral de Notre Dame, I sat waiting to see my sister. We, the cockatrice, had an intuition that enabled us to feel another cockatrice nearby, especially a sibling. I felt nothing. Was it because children no longer believed in us or needed us? I couldn't figure it out! Maybe I'd missed a memo sent out to all cockatrices that would have read something like this:

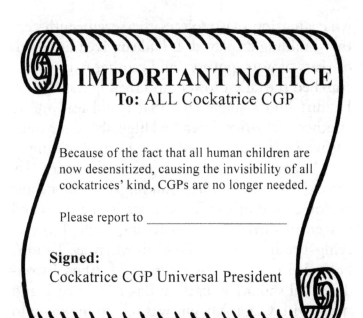

IMPORTANT NOTICE
To: ALL Cockatrice CGP

Because of the fact that all human children are now desensitized, causing the invisibility of all cockatrices' kind, CGPs are no longer needed.

Please report to _____

Signed:
Cockatrice CGP Universal President

Report to where? Somewhere I don't know! Where did everyone go?

The notice would have had information telling us what to do in the event that every human ceased to believe in the living cockatrice.

I had never understood why humans felt internal panic until then. I think some called it anxiety. Oh, and it didn't feel good. It made me feel jittery, like when I drank too much soda or coffee—but never too much cocoa drink. I needed to look, search every corner of the cathedral. Maybe Pia had left a clue.

Not a single photograph of the beautiful cathedral allowed someone to fully comprehend what amazing masterpieces the seventeenth-century building displayed. It had survived hundreds of years of wars, poverty, and mother nature. As I searched the tallest towers and the highest steeple, I didn't find a single clue that could lead me to another cockatrice. I perched high above the tourists who gazed up at the beauty of the building.

Masterpieces of carvings and statues lay throughout the entire building. Some people explored, and others found seats in the pews and prayed in silence. I sat, watching as the bus carrying Brody and his family drove away. I didn't know if I could follow them any further. I wondered if I should go back to Basel or go back and speak with Clara. My gut was telling me to go to the Cave Historique des Hospices, the next tour stop for Brody's family.

The Cave Historique des Hospices reeked of fermented grapes, dust, mold, and wood. The wine cellar was a dark and musty old place that screamed *danger* to anyone with allergies. I found Brody and kept my eye on him, thinking of how his body had reacted in the Black Forest and wondering what all the mold there would do to him. At least we were physically in a hospital basement in case of another emergency.

After the grape juice tasting, Brody and Bryant giggled and shared with each other how lucky they were not to have to taste the old smelly wine. I noticed Bowen making some human tourist friends his own age. He hung out with them, taking selfies with the barrels and pretending to drink the wine from the empty wine glasses.

Brody and Bryant went off to explore the cellar, sizing up the wine barrels that towered over them. The barrels were a few hundred years old, and some held the original wine made all those years ago. Most of the tour group was down the dark hall smelling the oldest of the wines. I saw Brody's little brother, Bryant, having a hard time. It looked like someone or something had taken his breath away.

I heard him think, "I am so tired."

Dashing toward the wall, I noticed everyone's eyes on Bryant, who was lying on the floor. I retrieved a heart portable defibrillator and made it fall to the ground, hoping someone would notice it.

Everyone rushed around the small boy lying on the concrete floor. A man in the group announced himself as a doctor, asking for everyone to step away. People gave him room, and he moved around, checking for a pulse, when Bryant woke up and seemed completely fine.

Bowen and Brody stood behind the crowd. Their skin seemed too pale, their hearts raced, and their eyes blinked away fear. I flew onto Brody's little shoulder and whispered in his ear, "Bryant will be fine. I promise you."

"He's right. Bryant will be fine," Bowen added.

Brody gulped, his eyes swollen as he nodded his head. Bravely, he said, "Thank you."

I froze like the statue in Basel! Did I just hear Bowen say, "He's right?"

Who's right? Did he hear me?

I also wondered why a little boy would need a machine that typically most old people needed. Bryant had gotten back to his normal self, and no one had to use the portable defibrillator on him, but I wondered why I thought he needed one? Maybe my senses were all wacky because my mind was preoccupied with finding my siblings. That could have been it.

Wait! I heard Bryant think... "I am so tired."

I followed the group back to the *Ama Kristina*. While in their cabin, I hid in the pile of dirty laundry and listened to the family talk about the day.

Meanwhile, I still wondered who Bowen was talking about. Did I hear him right? Did he say, "He's right?"

CHAPTER TWELVE

Brody

ALL FIVE OF US SAT in our cabin and talked about the day. Without a doctor's official diagnosis, Mom and Dad said Bryant might have HCM like me, but we wouldn't know until he saw a specialist and for now, we have to be cautious and treat Bryant basically like me.

"You will be okay, Bryant. Maybe you can find a hobby like I did, like playing the piano," I said. I tried to be optimistic about having HCM, especially since Bryant needs to know everything will be okay. Lots of people live to be old with it!

The bummer was that he really loved his soccer team, but maybe he would find something else he loved even more. He will have more time to play his guitar, and he can go golf with us.

"We all know his limitations, and once we get home, Bryant will go see Brody's heart doctor, a cardiologist, right away," Mom added, after asking him if he felt well enough to go to the concert that night.

Yes, of course he feels fine. I only know I have HCM because a doctor told me or when my heart races or I feel faint. Most of the time, I don't remember I have it and people around me sure don't know I have it. That is, until Mom asks me if I am okay over and over again! I know she worries, but I am fine!

Bryant had known of my heart condition forever, but it was still hard news to take, even if it was not official. He knew his life would change drastically, as mine had a couple years before. It was not fun! It was one of those "underlying conditions" that most people didn't know they had. I think about one in 500 people around the world had it. I had always felt very lucky we knew about HCM. I felt completely "normal," like I had before my diagnosis, and I could do most everything anyone else could, but with caution.

After Mom and Dad left our cabin, Bryant whispered to me, "Your creature friend, he was there with me!"

I stared at him for a moment, and my eyes darted around the room as if looking for answers. I didn't know how to feel or what to think, but I found myself whispering back to Bryant, "His name is Cody. He's a cockatrice, and I believe he is your friend too."

Bryant giggled, and we got ready for dinner.

We enjoyed whispering and sharing our secret "Cody" with one another at dinner, while Mom and Dad had to answer several questions from other passengers about Bryant passing out. After dinner, everyone had been invited to a private once-in-a-lifetime concert at St. Thomas Church. Daniel Maurer was an international award-winning organist, and he was also a professor of organ and improvisation at the Strasbourg Conservatory and Strasbourg Superior Music Academy. I was very impressed, and Bryant and Bowen thought it was very cool too.

We made our way to the church, noticing the large red sandstone bricks that led up to the first tower—or steeple—built in 1196, but it took more than 300 years to complete. As we walked inside the entrance, we were introduced to Professor Maurer and his wife. We walked around and saw a choir organ built in 1905. The coolest thing we found was the nickel silver organ pipes lining a whole wall. Those pipes were for the organ that Mozart had played in 1778.

We wandered around the church before the concert began. Bowen pointed out the medieval stained-glass windows and the marbled tomb sitting on stone, featuring carvings of lions. Bryant spotted the mosaic-like wall art of Fresco of Saint Michael. I was impressed with the tall marble columns and archways that framed the interior rooms. Professor Maurer appeared in the balcony above, waved, and quickly disappeared again.

Bryant and I sat with Cody between us, but I was not sure Cody knew we could see him. We waited for the concert and heard what sounded like a breath of air being sucked out from the building, followed by a shudder of deep rich sound that filled the whole church. Deep low tones and vibrant chords—the best of J. S. Bach and Mozart—sent goosebumps up and down my arms. I had to point out my goosebumps to Bryant, and he then pointed to his arms, where the little hairs were standing straight up.

Cody's feathers ruffled, and Bryant and I had to hold our laughter as we watched the little cockatrice's feathers fluff up while he shook. The usher came to show us the way up the stairs, where we were able to see Professor Maurer working peddles, pulling cords, and pressing keys. All four limbs were pumping, and it seemed like some old-fashioned exercise machine.

"It's brilliant," Bryant said. "Since I can no longer play sports, I will start playing more instruments."

I smiled at Bryant, thinking of how brave he was. After the concert, everyone was rushed back to the *Ama Kristina* for an on-time departure. The Once Upon the Rhine cruise guides welcomed us back, and they invited everyone to learn how to make macarons as the ship made her way farther down the Rhine River.

Once we were in the cabin, Bryant asked, "If Cody is a real cockatrice, why can't anyone else see him?"

Bowen shrugged. "I'm not saying I can see him. I think it's crazy, but if you two get caught talking about him, people are going to think you're crazy."

Bryant and I sat down on the bed, placed our macarons on the bedside table for Cody to enjoy, and went to sleep.

CHAPTER THIRTEEN

Cody

I WALKED BACK AND FORTH ON the small
balcony outside the cabin. Even though I
wanted so badly to make macarons with the
boys, I had lots to sort out.

In all the years I'd been a CGP, I'd never had
two kids in the same family, not ever, but possibly three kids in the same family—at the same
time—saw me. I was still not convinced that
Bowen saw me. Either way, I had two guardian
children, and that was crazy enough. One guard-

ian child is all I have ever had at once. It's in the CGP manual—well, it would be if we had one. And these are American children. They will be leaving Europe soon. What do I do then?

"Our next stop is Heidelberg, and my brother Sem should be near the palace."

Why did I feel like I was talking to myself all the time? At least I didn't feel the urge to count, but the pacing was wearing my little rooster feet out! It felt like something was poking me, nudging me, pushing me to continue the quest, even though I should have been in Basel. I decided I would continue on to Heidelberg. I would continue down the Rhine River aboard the *Ama Kristina*.

I watched the three boys sleep, wondering if I'd had the fifty years off to prepare me for the new adventure. But it didn't make sense. Why was I one of the last cockatrices? At the very least, why couldn't I find everyone? If my brother Sem wasn't in Heidelberg, I would have to go back to see my sister Clara in the Black Forest and speak with her.

I needed answers, and I needed them soon! I looked at Brody's face and knew he was the one, but then there were Bowen and Bryant. I was so confused.

The mixed-up voices I heard in Basel, it was all three of the boys talking and thinking at one time.

I slid open the sliding glass door to the balcony, fluttered through, and closed the door as softly as possible, flying into the night sky in search of answers.

CHAPTER FOURTEEN

Brody

A FLICKER OF A LIGHT TWINKLING through the shades woke me from a sound sleep. I slid out of bed and softly opened the sliding door, stepping out onto the balcony. Looking out as the land slowly drifted past, the soft breeze felt good.

Where does Cody sleep? Where does he go off to in the middle of the night? Is he going to stay with us the whole Rhine River adventure?

I looked up to the stars as they danced across

the sky. I placed more cookies onto the balcony's table for Cody, then slipped back inside the cabin and found my bed once again.

Morning came quickly, and as we made our way to the meeting area on deck, we were greeted by a friendly "*guten morgen*" from the guides. They wore color-coded shirts and filed off the *Ama Kristina* to board the buses. One bus of adventurers traveled to Mannheim, Germany, to visit museums and the Porsche and Mercedes-Benz automakers. Dad and Bowen had eagerly boarded the Mannheim adventure bus for the hour-plus drive to see the cool sports cars. They were dreaming of taking at least one back to America with us, I was sure.

Bryant, Mom, and I are with the other adventurers, going to Heidelberg to see the Heidelberg Palace. Heidelberg, what a fun word to say. The adventure guides supplied the music on the bus, keeping all of us laughing. They played the song by Peggy March, "Memories of Heidelberg," released in 1966, over and over again over the bus's speakers. It became well known as they repeated it. Randomly, someone would break out in song, like a musical, and everyone sang and laughed, especially Mom.

Mom gasped when she caught sight of the steeply sloping hill, and our bus's outside wheels hung off the ledge of the narrow and winding road. Everyone on the bus leaned toward the hill, and after every fifty yards or so, the bus would have to maneuver around a hairpin corner. We would then switch sides and lean into the hill again. Finally, the bus ended the roller-coaster ride at the Heidelberg Palace. The adults cheered and clapped for the bus driver not letting the bus topple down the hill.

The Schloss Heidelberg Palace ruins adventure group was shown around by a professional tour guide dressed in ghostly garb from the seventeenth century. Our ghostly guide had a fantastic haunting and airy voice. She introduced herself and invited the group on a trek back in time with her.

"The palace was first built in 1214, much like other fortresses and homes of royalty." The ghost waved her hand in the direction of one of the towers. "The palace grew, and with every new owner, they would add a new section, a new tower, a ballroom, or even an auditorium."

She waited for everyone to take in the view, and we followed her through the palace.

"This was one of Europe's largest palaces, and its last expansion was in 1650. It sits on a hill above the city of Heidelberg, and as you can see, on a beautiful day like today, we can see all the way to the next city. The palace was practically demolished by the French in both the Thirty Years' War and the Nine Years' War, but most of the building's walls are intact, and even the statues seem to be in perfect shape." The ghost added to her monologue by moving her hands in slow-flowing waves, pointing here and there while carrying on about the unique Romantic Renaissance structure. Cody appeared behind her, and he watched her as she weaved back and forth.

Bryant and I had our eyes glued on Cody. As we watched, Cody dramatically pulled a pretend sword from his sheath, flew up to the statue that was high up on the wall, bowed, and started a duel. He dashed back and forth, ducking and swaying, before suddenly halting. He flung his head up as if in pain. Pretending to be stabbed, he twisted and moaned, slowly falling to his pretend death. Seconds later, he began new improvisations as he turned himself into a king, a ruler; he puffed his little chest out and used his tail to gesture across his throat, mimicking "off with your head."

Cody then hovered close to our ghostlike tour guide's head. He dashed to the next open area in the garden, then flew back to another unique and old statue for yet another duel, acting out each scene the tour guide told.

Bryant and I couldn't contain our laughter, and we mocked a sword fight of our own, falling to the ground ourselves and crying from laughter.

The ghostly tour guide floated away from the group, wishing everyone well and a safe journey home. Mom led us down the steep hill, down hundreds of steps to the city of Heidelberg, and across a bridge over the Neckar River. There, we found a place where we could view—as Mom called it—"the Romanic Renaissance structure."

She referred to the Heidelberg Palace, which sat in the deep green forest on the north side of Königstuhl hill.

The bright sun directly above made it almost impossible for Mom to take pictures, but the sun's positioning made her realize we were late for lunch. We located a small café and ordered pizza and schnitzel, and after, we walked the carless street and found stores filled with treats. There were so many new candies and cakelike things I had never seen before, like gummies in pizza shapes and other flavors, like beef and beer. Cody clutched his beak with his little foot, warning us off the beer-shaped gummies.

"Yuck," I said in disgust, pointing at the small beer-bottle-shaped gummies Mom picked.

Bryant and I chose gummy pizza and a gummy bear just to keep it real. We purchased pastry dough balls called snowballs and quickly met up with the rest of the tour group to ride the bus back to the *Ama Kristina*.

We put our candy loot in the cabin before Bryant and I put on our swimsuits and headed off to the pool with a few other kids. As the hot afternoon sun lowered behind the hills, the other kids left the pool, allowing Cody to join us. He splashed and showed us his tricks and dives. Once Bowen and Dad arrived, we left the pool and heard all about Dad and Bowen's tours. I was a bit jealous of the free toy car Bowen had received from the exotic car museum tour, but we had our own unique adventures topped off with gummy bear and snowball treats.

At dinner, all the adventure guides were referring to the Porsche and Mercedes adventure tour as the Oprah Winfrey tour. Kolin, the adventure guide from Germany, didn't understand the joke, but the others waved their hands and pointed at guests while shouting, "And you get a car, and you get a new car!"

The little toy car was not as glamorous as an Oprah giveaway, but everyone laughed except Kolin, who was frustrated at not knowing this Oprah person. After dinner, we went to the cabin where I shared half of my snowball pastry treat with Bowen. I left some for Cody, whom I hadn't seen since the pool, on the nightstand.

CHAPTER FIFTEEN

Cody

ONE OF MY CGP POWERS was the keen ability to sense if and when my guardian child was in danger, even from miles away. So, if in fact Brody was my guardian child, I could search for my brother Sem and be able to take care of Brody—although not as easy, it was not impossible. Years ago, there were so many of us that if I needed to take off for a little while, another CGP was nearby to stand in until I came back.

It had been about ten years since I had seen

Sem, and he was also waiting for a new guardian child to find him, but his former guardian child had aged out of needing a CGP a few years prior to our encounter. He had a hard time leaving little Lena because she was so young when she decided she was "too old" for a make-believe creature that no one else saw or believed in. It seemed peer pressure had ended Sem and Lena's CGP-Guardian child relationship, and Sem had taken it hard. When Sem came to see me in Basel, I was in no mood to help. At the time, I hadn't been "seen" by a child in forty years, and I wasn't in the mood to be consoling someone else.

When I was at the Heidelberg Palace with Bryant and Brody, I felt no other cockatrice around, but I thought I should search a little harder before giving up on seeing Sem. I flew across the Neckar River and soared around the Thingspiele, an outdoor amphitheater built on the mountain and nestled within the trees. They had used large stones to make seats, which encircled the stage down the hill, for hundreds of people. There, people enjoyed reality beyond reality.

I thought if Sem were hanging out anywhere in Heidelberg and wasn't around the castle, it would be there, but I felt nothing, not even Sem. I decided to head back to the *Ama Kristina* to figure out my next plan. I thought I should go back to see Clara, but something nagged at me to continue with the river cruise. My intuition was typically spot on when it came to my guardian children, so I knew I'd better get back to the ship and stay around Brody.

As I approached the *Ama Kristina*, it flowed peacefully downstream, passing hundreds of castles and old churches that sat on hilltops and near the river's edge. Some white fluffy clouds dotted the sky, and the sun shone brightly as the family sat on the ship's deck chairs, watching the shoreline. As the *Ama Kristina* passed, someone on the ship's intercom announced the castles' names and their history.

A few hours later, a demonstration on making spaghetti ice cream was being given on the top deck. The ice cream was pressed through a spaetzle maker, making the ice cream look like spaghetti noodles. Strawberry sauce topped it for the marinara, and white chocolate bits replicated the Parmesan look. Watching the demonstration made me drool a little, and I was already plotting my move for the white chocolate bits they sprinkled on top.

It seemed everyone on the ship was in line for a serving, making the line unbearably long. Bowen was ahead of his family, surrounded by friends his age, while Bryant and Brody stood farther back in line. Their mom and dad chatted with friends. I hovered nearby, watching Bryant's eyes meet Brody's as if to speak silently to one another. They wondered what I was about to do.

That couldn't be right. These kids had figured out that I had a weakness for chocolate. I thought it was my imagination, but it wasn't! They knew I was drooling over the white chocolate.

I felt a ping of concern for Bowen, who received a bowl and picked up a spoon. I watched carefully as he started walking away, scooping a large bite toward his mouth. I dashed toward him, knocking the spaghetti ice cream from his hands.

Bowen cleaned up the mess, his face pink with embarrassment, and one of the guides offered him a new bowl. I knocked this one from his hand as well, and Bowen jerked his head around, looking straight at me. I was shocked. He saw me!

Brody grabbed a bowl of spaghetti ice cream without the strawberries and handed it to Bowen. "Aren't you allergic to strawberry sauce!"

"I am! I guess I thought a little wouldn't hurt," Bowen replied. "Mom has only given me raspberries because she said I am allergic to strawberries. How did he know?"

Mom showed up and looked at Bowen's bowl with a sigh. "Oh, good. You remembered not to eat strawberries!"

"Of course!" Bowen answered his mom while he looked in my eyes.

Why did Bowen forget something that big? I thought.

"I didn't think a little would hurt me," Bowen replied in his head but looking at me.

These American kids were a puzzle.

"Thank you, Cody," I heard Brody, Bryant, and Bowen think in unison.

No way! *This can't be possible! All three of them see me!*

I could hear all three boys in my head. Bowen might, or might not, be able to "hear me answer him."

I don't know what to do about this. It's insane! We cockatrices need a handbook! I needed to go, maybe count. Oh, no, not count. Maybe I need to sit and think about all of this.

The river water swiftly flowed past while I sat on the railing of the boys' cabin balcony. The bright stars and cool air would have been peaceful if my inner thoughts hadn't been wrestling inside my head. I hadn't even gotten any of the white chocolate bits they had been using for Parmesan cheese. I was getting quite attached to the kids, but they lived more than 4,400 miles away from Basel. If only I could have found another cockatrice to consult. They would know what I should do.

"What do I do? How would I get there when it's halfway around the world? Well, almost."

At my top speed of 100 miles per hour, I would have to travel about 4,400 miles to get to Atlanta, Georgia, USA (time = distance divided by speed). It would take me about forty-four hours to fly there if there wasn't any wind to consider. I paced back and forth on the little balcony, then decided to look for Clara. She was my best bet. I'd seen her, and I knew she was still around. I needed to go back to the Black Forest, find my sister, and find some answers.

Voices rattled in my head, and I paused to sort the words. I realized I could hear all three boys talking and thinking at once, and I couldn't seem to focus on one, but I heard Brody the clearest.

Three kids! At once!

CHAPTER SIXTEEN

Brody

THE *AMA KRISTINA* MANEUVERED THROUGH locks and tight winding bends of the Rhine. We sat and listened to stories over the intercom of two brothers—the sons of a king—who built their castles just out of reach from one another, fought over a girl, and never spoke again. Well, that's awkward.

Palaces, fortresses, and castles that were built from the 1200s overlooked the river from the top of the hillside. Miles and miles of vineyards lined the hills, some circling an entire estate. They looked like a huge bright green labyrinth that covered the hillsides. Most of the 20,000 castles were around 800 to 900 years old.

Along with castle facts and stories, other fun facts were indulged. We learned that it is bad luck to toast "cheers" with water, so we kept a soda or juice nearby when eating in Europe, as there always seemed to be a toast to cheer to. We learned that the first book ever printed came from Germany, and the longest published word is seventy-nine letters long—it was in the *Guinness Book of World Records* in 1972. The only other word I knew that was close was in Icelandic and sixty-four letters long: *vaðlaheiðarvegavinnuverkfærageymsluskúraútidyralyklakippuhringur*. I learned that when reading the *Iceland: The Puffin Explorers* series of books, but I still have no idea how to say it.

Our next day would be spent in Cologne (Köln), Germany. I couldn't wait to visit the world-famous chocolate factory. Meanwhile, Bowen, Bryant, and I swam in the small pool, playing games in the shaded lounge chairs. Mom and Dad visited with adults, and Mom took pictures as our ship traveled the Rhine River.

"Brody, have you seen Cody today?" asked Bryant.

"I haven't seen him all day," I answered, wondering where he was.

"Maybe he went home. We are getting far from Basel, you know," Bowen chimed in.

"I thought you didn't believe in him or didn't want to see him anymore," I responded.

"I am not going to tell anyone because they would think I am crazy, but after he sort of reminded me of my allergies, I think he's kind of cool. I like the little guy," Bowen replied.

"Why is he invisible to everyone except for us?" I asked Bowen.

"No idea, but I think we hear him think," Bowen said, tapping his chin. "Or he might hear us think because it's not like we are talking with him. We just hear him, and he hears us. I do sound insane. This is really weird."

Bryant jumped in and said, "Maybe no one else in the world has a cockatrice as a friend!"

"At least his stare doesn't kill us like in all the games with mythological creatures," Bowen added for good measure.

Mom called us out of the pool. It was time to get ready for dinner. Back at the cabin, there was no sign of Cody. I left some cookies on the bedside table just in case he came back while we were out.

There wasn't much chatter at the dinner table besides Mom and Dad talking to their new friends. I watched as Bowen and Bryant looked around and even snuck a peek under the table a time or two looking for Cody. All three of us seemed to miss him, but we knew he could go back to Basel. It wasn't like he's ours, and he was definitely not a pet. We couldn't wait to get back to our cabin, but when we arrived, Cody wasn't in the cabin either. We even tossed the dirty laundry pile to see if he was hiding. When we went to bed, he was still nowhere to be found. We left the sliding door unlocked and hoped that wasn't the last time we would see Cody the Cockatrice. All three of us stared up at the ceiling in the cabin as we tried to fall asleep. Hours crept, and at any little noise, I jumped up to see if it was Cody. My eyes eventually burned, and I let my dreams drift in.

The morning was dull, and there was even a feeling of melancholy without Cody. As we made our way up the steps to the Cologne Cathedral in Köln, we adjusted our headphones and the volume on our handheld radios, with the occasional glance or two extra for our little friend.

Danny, our guide, pointed at the cathedral and talked about its history. "They started building the cathedral in 1248 and finished in 1880. It wasn't a place to worship. It was a national monument that celebrated the newly-founded German empire. Sixty-one percent of Köln's built-up area was destroyed, and 20,000 citizens' lives were lost in World War II." Danny continued, "The cathedral wasn't damaged in the war because pilots needed to use it as a marker."

A buzz coming from our left side, reminding me of a kid mimicking an airplane engine, made me halt in my own footprints. Cody made an entrance like no other. He flew inside, shaping himself like an airplane and making the humming sounds of an engine. He made a slow turn, then mimicked missile sounds launching and exploding all around us. Bowen, Bryant, and I grinned at one another, trying not to howl with delight. It was hard to contain our happiness so no one would notice. While Danny spoke, we followed him and the group, entering the Cologne Cathedral as Cody acted out the history behind the magnificent Gothic cathedral throughout the tour inside, with Danny calling it the Kölner Dom. As we exited the Dom, we walked toward the cobblestone streets. It was amazing how we could picture the past hundred years or so through Cody's memories. We were hungry for more, but food sounded good as well.

We stopped for pretzels after leaving the cathedral. Walking on cobblestoned streets past churches, we learned that the word Kölsch has two meanings. It was what the Germans called their language, and it was also the word for beer. It was the only language one could drink.

Cody landed on my head and hopped with excitement, his thoughts going to the Chocolate Factory Museum. Tears flowed from Bryant's eyes. He couldn't contain his laughter any longer as he watched the cockatrice hop and frolic upon my head.

"What is so funny?" asked Mom.

Bryant and I stared at Bowen, almost in a panic.

"Brody's hair," exclaimed Bowen.

Mom turned and looked at it, her mouth quirking in a smile. "Ya, it is really messy."

Everyone nodded in agreement.

Bryant, Bowen, and I looked at one another, relieved.

We continued down the road, eventually reaching our destination. Cody fluttered and spun, whiffed the air with his beak, and flew off without us. We entered the chocolate museum and started reading more about the cacao plant, seeds, and harvesting. Cody was nowhere around but we knew he couldn't be far from the cocoa. The pictures and machinery brought everything that Stephanie had told us to life. The tiny teacups were smaller than I had imagined, and the plants were more like trees rather than the bushes I'd envisioned.

When we rounded the corner into the factory section of the building, we saw the line for the free chocolate samples. A long machine mixed chocolate, and it looked like thick chocolate milk. It then flowed through some pipes, and the chocolate shot into little mold trays, shaping it into small squares. The trays rotated around and around and shook, trying to rid the chocolate of air bubbles.

Once cooled, the trays of chocolate were

flipped over, and the chocolate squares fell out, waiting to be sorted into a line. Most of the squares went into a box, but every few seconds, if a button was pushed, one piece would come out a side slot.

The line wasn't moving, and people complained that this side of the machine was broken. My gut told me something was off. Although difficult to explain, I started to "feel" Cody, and he was extra happy. I walked toward the machine to see what was happening while everyone else stood in line.

Cody had tucked himself away inside the machine. As the machine's lever would drop the piece of chocolate out of the slot, Cody would snatch it up before it reached anyone's hand.

"Noooo," I said, wagging my finger at Cody.

The tips of Cody's feathers turned bright pink, and his chocolate-smeared beak shook. Cody dashed away, and he later appeared as we eyed the rows of chocolate in the museum's store. Dad carried the shopping basket, and we were allowed to choose four chocolates. I noticed Cody adding several more without anyone seeing him.

The lady at the counter was putting the chocolates into a bag when we heard the announcement that our bus had arrived. Dad quickly paid for our chocolate, not questioning the extras, and rushed us out to catch the bus.

When we arrived back at our ship cabins, we

dropped off the bags of goodies and went to the top deck. We hadn't noticed that Cody never exited the cabin.

CHAPTER SEVENTEEN

Cody

I SAT ON THE PATIO AS the *Ama Kristina* motored quietly downstream, watching Köln disappear. My heart thumped fast, and my feathers tingled at the thought of the past week and hearing Brody, Bryant, and Bowen laugh. It was wonderful to feel alive again.

I may have been the luckiest cockatrice alive. I hadn't found *a* guardian child. I had found *three*! Not only could I protect them from the world, but I could help them cope with their medical issues. They needed me. I was sure of it. At least,

I thought they needed me. The Rhine River ran into the North Sea, and the *Ama Kristina* would be there tomorrow. I only had a short time to figure out what to do when they boarded their plane back to the United States.

As I unwrapped the chocolate, I took a deep sniff. My leg shook excitedly, anticipating the rich wonderful taste of chocolate. I thought back on my conversation with Clara. She hadn't been very helpful in telling me what to do, but one thing was for sure: all the cockatrices were vanishing.

She kept herself busy and had been lucky to find guardian children steadily for all those years. She told me the others weren't so lucky.

We said our goodbyes, but before I left, she said, "I would not pass up an opportunity such as this one. Three boys and a chance to go to the United States of America. I think I would go, Cody, but that's just me. Whatever you do, be safe, and know I will always love you, my brother."

If I decided not to go, I would stop to see her on my way back to Basel.

I looked at my reflection in the sliding glass door. The ruby chocolate looked like lipstick on my beak, but I didn't care. I simply loved all chocolate. My thoughts soon blurred. I could hear faint laughter coming from the three American boys as I drifted off to sleep.

The *Ama Kristina* arrived in Amsterdam, the Netherlands, before dawn. We were definitely not in Basel anymore. I was not sure if it was simply an extra hot summer day or being in the city of Amsterdam, but this city sure welcomed the adventurers with its city noise and thick muggy air.

I watched as people disembarked. Everyone was reminded of the possible danger of simply walking on the bike paths.

The guide said, "Please, no one step inside the bike lanes."

As if on cue, a dozen bikes sped by like they had motors, making the warning ever so real. Bike transportation was a part of living in the city, and their marked off paths were only for bikes.

It was the last full day on the *Ama Kristina* with the amazing Once Upon the Rhine cruise guides. The thought made everyone sad, but on our way to the Van Gogh Museum, the guides helped by engaging the group with bits of facts while we explored the Amsterdam canals.

Bikes and water taxis were Amsterdam's lifeline, and we traveled through one of the 165 canals that ran through the 800-year-old city. The boat passed beautiful ancient churches and went under the most beautiful bridges, making its way through tunnels and deeper into the heart of the city.

Everyone seemed amazed by the slanted fronts of all the homes. Every home or structure slanted outward and pointed to the road. We saw a pully system used so they could lift heavy objects, furniture, or even pianos up, bringing them in through large windows upstairs.

The three boys most enjoyed looking at all the houseboats that were tied to the canal walls. Some looked like houses that floated, some were old broken-down boats that people lived on, and some had gardens on their decks. One boat had a child napping, others had people cooking over a stove or sitting in their bathrobes while drinking their morning coffee, and someone had forgotten to shut their curtains. This was definitely an interesting way to see into the lives of the people who lived in Amsterdam.

As I watched Bowen, Brody, and Bryant talking to their parents and listening to the history and stories of Amsterdam, I realized I needed to go find my brother Finn. Instead, I told myself

I would look for him later. I didn't want to miss seeing the Van Gogh Museum.

When the canal boat docked, the group disembarked and crossed a narrow street, making their way into the Van Gogh Museum. Everyone on the tour had to leave their backpacks in a locker before entering.

Bowen whispered to Brody, "Like we would try and put one of these huge paintings in our backpack?"

Brody giggled and placed his headset over his ears to listen to the tour guide.

"Van Gogh paintings hold the answer to whom Vincent Van Gogh was. We just have to look harder at his paintings and sketches for the answers." The guide walked ahead of our group, weaving her way through what seemed to be hundreds of people packed inside each room.

"I could tell you who he was without looking at his paintings." Bowen said. "He was an artist from the late 1800s who painted several self-portraits, even after he cut his own ear off."

Bowen didn't know anyone could hear him, but as several people turned his direction, his face turned a bright shade of red.

"Yes, but did you know he painted at least twenty-five self-portraits while in Paris, not because he was vain. He painted them because he was too poor to hire a model, and he wanted to practice painting portraits." The guide continued saying, "He wrote on the back of each painting, unknowingly naming each self-portrait. This is how Van Gogh was able to give us clues about the kind of person he was. Like this one." She pointed to the painting on the next wall. "Vincent wrote a letter to his brother, Theo, saying, 'I retain all good hope' after he cut his ear off."

The guide slid from room to room. Their mom and dad followed closely, but they kept their eyes on all three of the boys while climbing up the steps to the next section of treasures. Brody, Bowen, and Bryant weaved through the thick crowd, which obscured their view of most of the paintings. When they made it to the front, the three boys studied each painting and watched me act out the next possible thoughts of Van Gogh. It was an interesting game of charades, trying to have them guess Van Gogh's mood while he painted each masterpiece. Too bad Vincent Van Gogh didn't know they were masterpieces when he was alive.

The guide continued her lecture, "More than 1,000 paintings, drawings, and letters are in this museum. This is the largest Van Gogh collection in the world. Seeing these paintings, can anyone guess what his favorite color was?"

Brody yelled, "Yellow?" He also turned a lovely shade of red after realizing he had yelled.

"Why, yes! He loved the sun and the color yellow. One of his most well-known self-portraits is him wearing his yellow straw hat. In Vincent's painting, *The Sunflowers*, the vase, the table, the wall, and of course the flowers are yellow."

"He loved yellow or no one else wanted to use it," Bryant chimed into the guide's monologue.

"Maybe it was!" answered the tour guide. "We have some smart young people on this tour with us today," she said into her microphone for everyone in the group to hear.

The boys turned their headset volumes down and snuck off to the sunflower wall painted near the staircase so people could take selfies with it, and their mom followed them. The boys took selfies and mimicked Vincent Van Gogh's poses and expressions while laughing at each other and at me. Soon, their mom led them back to the front, where the group had gathered. Everyone found their backpacks, exited the museum, and walked to their next adventure.

CHAPTER EIGHTEEN

Brody

S TEPPING INTO THE CANAL BOAT, we noticed the easels, paints, and paint brushes on all of the tables. After we realized we would paint something Van Gogh, we rushed to the easel with the picture of the painting we wanted to try. I chose Van Gogh's *Fishing Boats on the Beach at Les Saintes Maries-de-la-mer* from 1888. At least, that's what had been written on the back of the picture. Bowen chose one of the self-portraits without the ear, and Bryant chose *The Starry Night*—both from 1889.

We dove into painting. We didn't even notice

which paintings Mom and Dad had chosen to paint because we were having so much fun. The canal ride was quiet, and everyone on the little canal boat was fixated on their canvases. It was a lot different than any art class at school. We had to stop painting when the canal boat became dark, so we paused to look around. As the canal boat exited the dark tunnel, work resumed. Bryant had difficulty with his stars swirling and asked for help, but then I noticed Cody.

Cody saw Bryant's frustration, and he was greeted by Bryant's whisper, "Where did you come from?"

Cody cocked his head and motioned for Bryant to move his paintbrush over. Cody dipped his feet into the paint and spun like an Olympic skater. Bryant giggled and was amazed at how his painting transformed.

A moment later, the art teacher walked past Bryant and said, "Nice brushwork, young man!"

Bowen looked over and noticed the cool work, asking, "Bryant, how did you do that?"

Bryant shook his head to his left, and Cody peeked out from behind the easel. All three of us laughed. Cody jumped over to my painting and pranced through the fresh paint on the palette, beginning a little dance of his own and making the sea and wind appear to drift off the canvas.

"You have a nice brush technique too, young man." The voice came from behind me, causing me to jump off my seat.

I looked down and noticed Cody's feet, wondering if anyone could see them while covered in paint. It's paint—real paint—so it's possible anyone could see his feet. Cody made eye contact with me and read my mind, and I moved my body between the instructor and the easel so she couldn't see Cody's feet, just in case.

Cody dove behind the easel, and his sudden move caused a domino effect. All four easels on the table crashed down. Like a ripple effect, yellow and brownish paint water splashed everywhere.

After the commotion, we heard the art teacher say, "If you don't laugh, you might cry. Isn't that how the saying goes?"

Everyone giggled to ease the tension in the canal boat. As the group disembarked the painting cruise workshop, it was clear who was infected by the paint fiasco and who wasn't. Pant seats were covered in wet brownish water, making it look like everyone on board had had an accident in their pants. A very bad accident!

Bowen, Bryant, and I felt horrible, but at the same time we couldn't stop our bodies from convulsive movements trying not to laugh out loud. Mom and Dad apologized to everyone, and they made us apologize as well.

"I am sorry," Cody whispered fearfully before fleeing the scene of the crime.

We arrived back in our cabin, expecting to see Cody half hiding and fearful of what trouble he had caused us, but he wasn't around. Not knowing when Cody would leave to go back to Basel was wearing thin on all three of us. We were getting used to Cody being around, and I could feel a hint of worry. What if we would never see him again? A gloom rushed over me like a thunderstorm shutting down the Fourth of July fireworks, closing time at a theme park, or worse.

***

Bowen, Bryant, and I were in our cabin packing our suitcases after washing all the paint off of us. We would transfer to a hotel in the morning and would fly home the very next day.

"Today was the best day ever—worst day ever! We had a blast in Amsterdam, but it was our last night on the ship, and will we see Cody again?" I said out loud to Bowen and Bryant and a little talking to myself. They both shook their heads in agreement.

I learned that I was not a 'Van Gogh,' but with practice I could be. I laughed at the thought. Van Gogh had to practice a lot. He must have loved painting, but he wasn't famous until after he died. I wondered if Vincent Van Gogh's parents had been disappointed with their son's decision to become an artist. Maybe that's why he had been so sad. Moms and dads were always proud of their children, if they were not, they were wrong. I wish he had a friend like Cody, but…well, maybe he did. Maybe that's why Cody could paint so well.

"Do you think Cody will come say goodbye to us tonight?" Bryant asked me.

"I hope he says goodbye, but he felt bad he caused all of that trouble on the art cruise today. Did you see everyone's pants? It looked like they…"

I couldn't finish the sentence, and at the thought, started laughing so hard I fell to the floor.

"Pooped their pants," Bryant said, as tears ran down his cheeks and he hysterically fell to the floor.

We had to contain all our thoughts on the way to dinner and while we ate so not to get hysterical in public.

After dinner, Mom and Dad came to our cabin to help us finish packing. Once we were done, we only had our clothes for the morning. We lay in our beds and stared up at the ceiling; all three of us were hoping for this trip not to end.

"I sure hope Cody comes to say goodbye," I whispered, hoping somehow he would hear.

When morning came, I jumped up and looked all around for Cody, but I didn't see him anywhere. We said our farewells to the guides, Jackson, Calli, Missy, Kolin, and Danny. As they dropped us off at the hotel, we had a hard time smiling, knowing our 'holiday' was over.

We headed to the Zaanse Schans windmills, where Mom couldn't wait to take some pictures, and Dad couldn't wait to sample cheese and see if it came close to his favorite Wisconsin cheese. Bowen wanted to take a bike ride around the meadow, and Bryant and I wanted to see how they made clogs. Wooden shoes didn't sound comfortable to me, but I believed painting would be involved. We stared out the taxi window as we left the city and crossed over bridges until we found ourselves on long strips of road with nothing but land on both sides.

On the right side of the car, a breeze was gently flowing over the green grassy meadow, and it kept the huge wooden windmill arms spinning. We stared outside the car window, pointing out which wooden house and windmill was painted in our favorite colors.

"I wish I could paint a picture as pretty as this," Bryant said.

"Why can't you?" Mom asked.

We exited the taxi and walked into a storybook scene. The wooden windmills and wooden houses lined the shore around the lake. Hand-painted signs for boat tours, clog decorating, and cheese-making demonstrations lined the walkway as we made our way into the unique little town.

Fluffy soft clouds dotted the bright blue sky as our reflections danced on the lake.

I looked at my reflection in the water more than once, hoping to see Cody's reflection looking back at me. I wondered if I would see him pop out of the water like a fish as he had in Basel. We walked past one of the mills and inhaled the fresh spices being ground inside. The smell suddenly made me hungry, and we all agreed to get fresh grilled cheese sandwiches made at the house.

Bryant was fascinated by the mill, where pigments were made. He wanted to buy all the paint colors they had. Bowen pleaded with Mom and Dad to rent bicycles, so Dad and Bowen took off down the bike paths through the nature trails. Mom stayed with us, purchasing gifts to take home, and we drank fresh-squeezed orange juice sold by a local teen.

Every place we had visited was a new adventure, and that visit ended with Bryant and me painting our clogs. It wasn't as fun without Cody, but they were small enough to fit Cody, and we laughed, picturing Cody wearing these clogs.

On the way back to the hotel, we sat in silence and continued watching the scenery pass our car windows.

We arrived back at the hotel room and pulled out our video games to occupy our time while Mom and Dad went to take a walk.

"I hate goodbyes," I said to Bowen and Bryant.

"Me too," my brothers answered.

Knowing we had made such a great friend, it was hard to say goodbye to Cody.

"I don't think goodbyes will be a problem because I think he has already headed home to Basel." I sighed.

"Not even a 'later, alligator,' 'in a while, crocodile?' Not even an 'out the door, dinosaur?' " asked Bryant.

"An 'out the door, dinosaur' would be kind of fitting for a cockatrice, don't you think!" Bowen said, trying to make us smile.

I already missed feeling the slight wavy movement of the *Ama Kristina*. I missed our adventure guides wishing us all a good night in three different languages. The night before was *goedenacht* (khoo-duh-nahkht), and that morning had been *goedemorgen* (khoo-duh-mawrghuh), *dank je* (dank ya), and *tot ziens* (toht-zeens), but good morning, thank you, and goodbye had seemed so final. Bryant yelling *nee* (nay) for nooooo and reaching back, as if not wanting to leave the ship, was actually funny. I think all of us felt the same way.

I wished we could fly back to Basel with the guides and start the river cruise all over again like the Once Upon the Rhine adventure guides did all summer long. Mom and Dad came back to the room and shut the window. I watched, knowing that Cody couldn't say goodbye unless he had some magical power to walk through a shut window or locked door.

CHAPTER NINETEEN

Cody

THE PAINT ON MY YELLOW feet had almost faded by the time I reached the North Brabant area where my brother Finn lived. It was in the south of the Netherlands where he had once long ago—in the late 1850s—been Vincent Van Gogh's CGP. Sharing stories with Finn had been a blast. We stayed up all night long, and he said that he too had helped little Vincent play with paints, but he had left long before he was a serious artist.

Finn was my only brother who looked just like me. The only slight difference was our claw colors, and with mine painted orange, we almost matched. He had also noticed that the cockatrice were almost gone. He knew some of the faeries had left for the countryside to live in the meadows, but the cockatrice had simply disappeared.

He reminded me of a story that had been told when we had been little and in training. The dragon-godparents had all vanished at one point, and they were eventually found in a land called Japan. Their trainers—or elders—were there, and they possibly had the answers. Although it could have been that as time passed, the world changed. Perhaps when we retired, that's when the place would be revealed.

Finn was helpful, but when I asked the hardest question of all, he only said, "The answer is inside you, and only you will know."

What's that supposed to mean? Am I "allowed" to go to the United States?

After Bowen, Bryant, and Brody, was I supposed to find someone new there?

Please don't make me count again, please don't make me count again, please don't make me count again!

I said goodbye to Finn and flew away. The morning sun had yet to crest the horizon. I flew over the roads and counted the cars' headlights.

"One, two, three."

Oh, wait. What direction should I fly? What way

*am I going? Do I go back to Basel or to Amsterdam
to find the boys?*

"Four, five, six."

I'll go back to say goodbye, at least.

"Seven, eight, nine…"

CHAPTER TWENTY

Brody

OUR BAGS WERE STUFFED AND ready to go. We had chocolates from Basel and Cologne, as well as Kugelhopf cakes and a stuffed Alsatian stork from Strasbourg. There were German Christmas ornaments, Heidelberg gummies, and a wooden nutcracker holding a Black Forest cuckoo clock. There were wooden clogs from Volendamh and five Van Gogh paintings that we had created on the little canal painting excursion. Souvenirs and trinkets stuffed our suitcases, almost busting the zippers and locks.

As we stood outside and waited for a ride to the airport, Bryant whispered softly to me, "Is he going to say goodbye?"

"I don't think he can, but I am sure he wanted to," I replied sadly.

Not only were we leaving Europe, but we were leaving our secret—our new friend—in Amsterdam, or in Basel, forever. The reality settled in, and my eyes burned at the thought of leaving.

We piled in the airport transport van and every turn the van made, I looked and searched for Cody. I sat and watched Bowen and Bryant do the same. Arriving at the airport, I thought he would pop up on someone's head in front of us or pretend to surf ride a rolling suitcase through the airport. The thought of him sneaking around the airport looking for cocoa made me smile. Before we boarded the plane, Mom and Dad tried to cheer us with one last cocoa treat for the plane ride home. It's not as if I didn't want the chocolate, it was the feeling of having chocolate without Cody that made me feel empty.

When we boarded the airplane, I watched as people below the plane loaded luggage onto the conveyer belt and avoided the family small talk. I found my seat, buckled my seatbelt, and said my goodbyes in my own special way, facing out the window. I couldn't stop that little tear as it rolled down my cheek during takeoff.

After the plane reached a safe altitude, I selected a movie to watch and put on my headphones. Midway through the movie I wasn't really watching, the flight attendant asked me for my drink preference. When she reached over to hand me my napkin and cookie, I noticed something odd on her shoulder. Little smudges of brown, maybe cocoa. Little Van Gogh swirls.

Before I could get a better look, the flight attendant was off to the next aisle.

"It couldn't be," I said softly.

Maybe I wanted to see Cody so badly that I was imagining things. I tried to focus back on the movie, but I finished my drink and drifted off to sleep.

I dreamt of Cody the Cockatrice, or perhaps I thought I was dreaming. I felt peace and somehow knew or felt that Cody was safe.

Bowen nudged me and Bryant poked me.

Why are they waking me?

I wanted to sleep off the pain of missing Cody, but as I opened my eyes and looked down to where Bryant and Bowen were pointing, I gasped.

Curled up, almost catlike on my lap, Cody the Cockatrice was sleeping.

I took the cocoa from my pocket and left it near Cody's head. Oh, how Cody loves his cah–cow! Bowen, Bryant, and I smiled at one another, and we couldn't wait for our next adventure to begin.

TO BE CONTINUED

Dear Reader:

We hope you enjoyed *Once Upon the Rhine*, book one in the Cody the Cockatrice series. We would love to hear your thoughts, so please return to your favorite online retailer to write a review and/or drop me a note at ra-anderson.com.

BOOK TWO EXCERPT

THE LAND OF VIKINGS & TROLLS

(Cody the Cockatrice Series Book Two)

The thumping within my ears was like a race-horse galloping in my veins. A few of my feathers fled from my body, upward as if to fly themselves. My mind fought within itself, wondering why I couldn't successfully sneak past those two warrior goddesses. Those felines should both be in the kitchen watching the boys' mom cook dinner or at least trying to annoy the boys while they worked on their homework. The rich cocoa fragrance taunted me. I could almost taste Mom's stash, made by Lindt, in her room. Her cocoa was tucked away somewhere close to her nightstand, maybe inside it. Mom had a love for the good stuff like I do. She kept it hidden from the boys, but I knew better. The aroma called to me! Even though I was invisible to her, I wasn't to everyone in the house. Athena and Mia, not the Greek goddesses, but these two furry critters that were house cats this family rescued. They left me alone for the most part but seemed very protective of

Mom's belongings, especially this bedside dresser. It sure would have been helpful if I were invisible to pets, especially these cats. Why couldn't I be invisible to animals instead of only humans who don't believe in me?

Securing myself out of reach from the two goddesses' dagger nails and mighty leaps was easy, but when I got close to cocoa, I threw caution to the wind. Sometimes I got distracted by the heavenly smell, my focus becoming blurred and anything possible. That's how close Athena and Mia were—even my feathers on my back fled my little body. Don't get me wrong, I am fierce as a dragon and magical as a faerie, but these two little goddesses could be toast and would need all of their nine lives trying to slay me. My hands are tied, my powers are useless, because Athena and Mia were family, and I was there to protect my people, and I guess, these little calico goddesses were included in the clan. I could outwait them. The sizzling of bacon beckons the colorful goddesses back to the kitchen, leaving me alone with creations from the chocolate manufacturer and inventor, Rudolph Lindt, a fellow Swiss native.

Hidden in Brody's room, I would hide some cocoa for later. I looked up on his wall in our bedroom to admire the painting he had done for me to help make this more my home too. Although summer is not over and I have overheard the parents, so I already knew our next adventure was coming soon.

Acknowledgments

To Todd, thanks for our adventure down the Rhine.

To Cody, Brody, and Zane for letting me channel their younger selves.

To Sharon, Rudy, Bill, and Mary, thanks for always believing in me.

To my favorite Fairy TripMother, Christy Shadday, for organizing such amazing adventures.

Thank you, Hannah Jones, for bringing Cody the Cockatrice to life.

Thank you, Lindsey Taylor, for creating the painting for Brody's room. She can be found on Instagram @lindseytaylorstudio for those interested in seeing more of her artwork.

Thank you to my editing team and book designers at IAPS.rocks.

&

A special thank you to Lisa at 4HCM.org for all the support you give HCM warriors.

About the Author

RA Anderson is a wanderer who has lived all over, from California to Belize, and currently, home is a town called Rome—in Georgia, that is! She grew up on horseback and sailboats, "the most amazing way to grow up!"

A lifelong passion for creative writing and photography became her life. Her award-winning photographs have been featured in table books, magazines, and front-page news, and her writing has been published in magazines, poetry books, young adult books and children's books.

Three boys—her heart and soul—call her Mom. She and her husband—"my strength and passion"—are recent empty-nesters, leaving them more time to travel.

"My life is full, colorful, and exhausting, and I wouldn't trade it for anything. However, people seem to think my most impressive accomplishment is that I know how to work the manual settings on a DSLR camera!"

https://ra-anderson.com/
https://www.facebook.com/raAndersonAuthor
https://www.instagram.com/ra_anderson_author/
https://twitter.com/Aruthanne

Books by RA Anderson

Once Upon the Rhine
(Cody The Cockatrice Series Book One)

The Last Crabtree Girl

Girl Sailing Aboard the Western Star

Puffins Take Flight
(Iceland: The Puffin Explorers Book 1)

Puffins Off the Beaten Path
(Iceland: The Puffin Explorers Book 2)

Puffins Encounter Fire and Ice
(Iceland: The Puffin Explorers Series Book 3)

Iceland: The Puffin Explorers Book of Fun Facts

If Pets Could Talk: A Service Dog

If Pets Could Talk: Dogs

If Pets Could Talk: Cats

If Pets Could Talk: Farm Animals

CPSIA information can be obtained
at www.ICGtesting.com
Printed in the USA
BVHW090108140722
641763BV00005B/9